"I never dreamed   exclaimed, gaping at Sie   orse
for having galloped ne   d sixteen fences. "He doesn't look like the same horse I
saw two weeks ago. He's running like he wants to."

"He *does* want to," Samantha said.

"What's next?" Mike asked.

"There's a novice steeplechase in Lexington at the
end of April," Samantha explained. "It's not a sanctioned meet, but we thought it would a good place to
start Sierra and give him some experience—if you
agree to running him," she added, anxiously watching Mike's face.

"Right here in town, huh?" Mike rubbed his chin
thoughtfully. "It sounds like a good opportunity for
him to prove himself. All right, why not? But I'll tell
you honestly that if I'm going to put any more time
and money into him, he's got to do well. This will be
his last chance. In fact, I was talking to a breeder in
Florida who might be interested in buying him for
stud if I decide to sell."

Mike's last words sent Samantha's heart plummeting to her feet. "The race is Sierra's last chance?" she exclaimed.

Collect all the books in the Thoroughbred series

Collect all the books in the Ashleigh series

coming soon*

THOROUGHBRED

SIERRA'S STEEPLECHASE

JOANNA CAMPBELL

HarperPaperbacks
A Division of HarperCollins*Publishers*

HarperPaperbacks   *A Division of* HarperCollins*Publishers*
                   10 East 53rd Street, New York, N.Y. 10022

Produced by Daniel Weiss Associates, Inc., 33 West 17th Street, New York, New York 10011.

First printing: December, 1993

Printed in the United States of America

HarperPaperbacks and colophon are trademarks of HarperCollins*Publishers*

20   19   18   17   16   15   14

IT'S GOING TO BE ANOTHER ONE OF THOSE WORKOUTS, Samantha McLean thought grimly as she rode Sierra onto the training oval at Whitebrook. They'd barely stepped onto the track when the high-spirited two-year-old Thoroughbred began to dance sideways across the harrowed dirt, gathering his muscles and kicking out. Samantha's legs were tight on the girth of the English saddle, and her fingers were wrapped in Sierra's mane. His bucks didn't even come close to unseating her, but his behavior was a bad omen. "Just quiet down and put in a decent workout for a change!" she ordered the colt.

Sierra gave another playful kick, bouncing them up the track, but when he finally realized Samantha was staying put, he snorted in disgust and started trotting up the dirt oval. Samantha knew the strong-willed colt was testing her. They played the same game nearly every morning. Eventually Sierra would

1

settle down, but not without giving her a hard time first.

The dark chestnut colt had trained so poorly earlier in the year that he'd already missed the chance to race during his two-year-old season. Since he was still training badly now, in October, it didn't seem as if he would be ready to race in Florida over the winter, either.

The sun was rising over the treetops of the Kentucky farm, highlighting the russet-and-gold leaves of fall. Samantha loved Whitebrook. The atmosphere was friendly and happy, unlike Townsend Acres, the huge breeding and training farm where Samantha and her father, Ian McLean, had lived before. Now Samantha's father worked as head trainer for Whitebrook's owner, Mike Reese. Samantha helped with the morning workouts and was exercise rider for Wonder's Pride, the magnificent Kentucky Derby and Preakness winner who was half-owned by Mike's girlfriend, Ashleigh Griffin.

She just wished that Sierra would put his mind to business and start training the way he was supposed to. She'd always had a special feeling for the colt and desperately wanted him to do well.

Samantha kept a firm grip on the reins as she warmed Sierra up at a trot. After circling the oval once, Samantha gave Sierra the signal to canter. Immediately he tried to lunge straight into a gallop. She held him with hands and arms that were strong from her three years of exercise riding high-strung racing Thoroughbreds. At nearly sixteen,

Samantha was assured and skilled in the saddle.

Sierra didn't like the restraint one bit. He fought Samantha every inch of the way as they finished lapping the mile track. Finally, as they passed the mile marker pole, Samantha crouched in the saddle and gave Sierra the rein he'd been fighting for. "Go!" she cried.

Thrilled to be getting what he wanted, Sierra exploded forward as if he'd been shot from a cannon. They swept around the first turn into the backstretch. Sierra's hoofbeats pounded on the dirt, and his powerful strides ate up the distance. His long mane whipped back into Samantha's face, and her own red hair flew out from beneath the back of her helmet as they surged along.

"Maybe this time I can keep you interested for more than half a mile," Samantha muttered as she kept the colt close to the inside rail for the run up the backstretch.

They'd barely gone half the distance of the backstretch when Samantha felt Sierra suddenly drop the bit. "No!" she cried angrily. "Don't start playing around again!" She kneaded her hands along the colt's neck, urging him to keep up the pace. But as he'd done in so many training sessions before, Sierra shortened his stride and started loafing.

"Come on! I know you can do it!" Samantha cried to the colt. "Do you want Mike to think you're a total failure?"

Sierra's ears flicked back, then pricked forward again, showing his disregard for Samantha's instructions. Instead of picking up the pace, he tossed his sleek head and tried sidestepping across the track. Samantha gritted her teeth and tightened her left rein, holding the colt firmly on course as they came around the turn toward the stretch at a dawdling and lazy gallop.

Samantha wanted to scream, and she knew that Mike, Sierra's owner and trainer, must be feeling the same disappointment. She glanced over at the opening to the oval, where Mike was standing with Samantha's good friend, Tor Nelson. Even from a distance, Samantha could see that they were frowning. When she passed the marker pole, Samantha stood in the stirrups, signaling the colt to drop back into a canter. She kept a firm hold on the reins, though—Sierra was unpredictable enough that he might suddenly decide to bolt forward up the track.

This time he obeyed, and Samantha slowed him further to a trot, then turned him and headed off the track. The beautiful colt tossed his head and pranced along with a springy, elegant step. He didn't seem at all concerned that he had put in another horrendous workout.

Samantha rode over to Mike and Tor. "As usual, I couldn't keep him going," she said. Her tone echoed her discouragement. "He decides that he's had enough running and just backs off. And it's not because he's tired."

Tor shook his blond head. "No, he definitely doesn't look tired."

Sierra was still full of energy, dancing his hindquarters around as Mike held him so that Samantha could dismount. Samantha looked Sierra over and saw that not a spot of sweat marred his gleaming liver chestnut coat. Sierra craned his head around to watch her as she pulled up the stirrups. Samantha was sure there was a glint of devilish glee in that look.

"Got your way again, didn't you?" she said to the colt. Frustrated as she was, she couldn't stay angry with Sierra for long. It was just so infuriating that he refused to work to his potential. "You know, when he puts his mind to it, he burns up the track," she said to Mike and Tor.

"I know," Mike answered wryly. "I timed that first half-mile. He did it in forty-five seconds—amazing time, if he'd kept it up. You don't want to know how slowly he ran the second half."

"I could feel it." Samantha groaned. "It was like we were moving in slow motion."

"Why do you think he's losing interest?" Tor asked.

Mike shrugged. "I don't know. I'm really stumped about his training. It's not that he doesn't have any talent. And he definitely has the right breeding. All of Maxwell's other foals have been training well, and Sierra's dam is a Secretariat mare. Her previous foals have all done well. I hate to say it, but I'm almost ready to give up on him."

"No, not yet!" Samantha cried. "He'll come around. He's only two. Maybe he's just a late bloomer. I'll put in some extra time working with him."

"I appreciate your wanting to help, Sammy," Mike said, "but with Pride working up to the Breeders' Cup in a couple of weeks, when are you going to *have* the time?"

"I can squeeze in an hour in the afternoons," Samantha said quickly. "And after the Breeders' Cup, Pride will be getting some time off. Maybe I could try working Sierra with a pace horse again."

"It didn't work the first time," Mike pointed out. "He was more interested in trying to bite a chunk out of the other colt's neck."

Tor walked over to Samantha's side. "I admit I don't know much about racing," he said to Mike, "but I do know jumping, and I saw Sierra clear the paddock fence last summer. Since he's already being trained to race, did you ever think of steeplechasing him? He might have the talent for it."

"I don't know anything about training a steeple-chaser," Mike answered, "and I don't have the facilities. If he fails on the flat, my only option is to sell him. I really don't need him for stud, and I frankly can't afford to hold on to any unnecessary stock. I suppose we could think of gelding him. That might settle him down, but I'd hate to geld a colt with his bloodlines. He could be a valuable stud to someone else."

"Let me just try working with him a little longer," Samantha pleaded. She understood Mike's position. He and his father had gradually built up Whitebrook to a successful training and breeding operation. They couldn't afford to hold on to horses that weren't earning some kind of return. Yet the fact that Mike was even considering selling Sierra came as a shock to Samantha—she had spent enough time working with the two-year-old to think that the colt had talent.

"If you can find the time, Sammy, go ahead," Mike told her. "I've got other two-year-olds that are really coming along, like his half sister, Ms. Max. I need to concentrate on getting those horses ready to race in Florida this winter. Maybe you can do something with Sierra." He didn't sound very optimistic.

Mike turned and headed off toward the barn that housed the horses in training. Sierra had been the last of the horses worked that morning. Mike and Mr. McLean had started at dawn, and now it was nearly seven thirty.

As Samantha and Tor led Sierra away from the oval, Mike's stable manager, Len, walked up with a lead shank. The old black man was a fan of Sierra's, too, and just as disappointed as Samantha and Mike that Sierra wasn't training well.

"So he threw in another dud," Len said as he clipped the shank to Sierra's bridle and rubbed the colt's nose. "Eh, there, no biting!" he warned the horse, "or I'll bite you right back." Sierra eyed him, but his lips stayed closed over his teeth. "Don't give up yet," Len said to Samantha. "I know it's hard being patient, but he'll smarten up."

Tor laughed. "Actually, I think his problem is that he's *too* smart. That's why he gets bored so easily and thinks up so many tricks to get his own way."

Len grinned. "You may be right about that. Isn't that so, young monster?" he added fondly to Sierra.

7

Len glanced at Samantha. "I cooled Pride out for you. He's back in his stall eating a hearty breakfast."

"Thanks, Len. I appreciate it."

"At least Pride put in a good workout this morning," the old man added. "Looks like he's all set for the Breeders' Cup. Can't believe the way he's come back after all those disappointments last summer. He sure showed them his stuff in the Gold Cup last week. I've got a feeling come Breeders' Cup day, it'll be two wins in a row."

"I hope so!" Samantha said. Samantha's favorite horse, Wonder's Pride, had been through a lot that year. Samantha had played a big part in Pride's training. She had been bitterly disappointed when Pride lost the third jewel of the Triple Crown, the Belmont Stakes, after winning the Kentucky Derby and Preakness. Then his co-owners, Ashleigh Griffen and Clay Townsend, had starting fighting over his training and race schedule. The colt had been affected by the tense battles over him and had put in four increasingly dismal races. Only when the fighting had finally stopped did Pride start winning again. "He's on his toes," Samantha said. "We're on our way to see him now."

"Well, let me get this guy walked and cooled out. See you later," Len said as he led Sierra away.

Samantha and Tor headed toward the training barn. Samantha was really pleased that Tor had come over to watch the morning workouts. Her best friend, Yvonne Ortez, had been taking jumping lessons from Tor at one of the Lexington riding stables. When Yvonne had introduced Samantha to Tor over a year before, Samantha had liked him right away. Over the past months, she and Tor had become increasingly closer, bonded by their mutual interest in horses.

"You know," Tor mused, "I really think Sierra could make a jumper. Racing over fences might keep him more interested, too."

"Maybe it would," Samantha said. "I always thought Sierra was special, but it's up to Mike to make the decisions. I'll try to think of something to get Sierra on track. I sure don't want Mike forced into selling him!"

As they walked into the barn, Samantha heard a welcoming whinny from farther down the aisle. She saw Pride's elegant chestnut head extended over his stall door and quickened her pace. "Yeah, boy, I'm finally coming to see you, but I can't stay long. I have to leave for school." When she reached the three-year-old colt's stall, she rubbed a loving hand over Pride's sleek neck. As usual, Sidney, one of the stable cats, was seated on the edge of the stall partition, grooming himself. The nearly grown white-and-black kitten had an unforgettable face, with black markings that came down around his eyes and over his nose and chin like a mask. He had an endearing personality to match his coloring.

"Hi, Sid," Samantha said to the cat as he rose on the narrow partition top and stretched. "Are you keeping Pride company?"

The kitten let out a rumbling purr as Tor picked him up and scratched his chin.

Wonder's Pride nudged Samantha gently with his

nose. "I haven't forgotten you, boy," Samantha said. "You put in a great workout for me this morning. We'll give you another one later this week, then you'll be flying to California with Ashleigh and Charlie."

"And a week later, you'll be flying out, too," Tor said.

"It's going to be incredible!" Samantha exclaimed, blushing under the gaze of Tor's bright blue eyes. "I've never been to the West Coast. And it's great that you and Top Hat are competing in a California show the same weekend. You can watch the Breeders' Cup with me. When are you and your father vanning Top Hat out?"

"Five days before the show," Tor answered easily. "We'll switch off with the driving, but we want to give ourselves extra time in case we have a breakdown or something."

Samantha glanced at her watch. "I'd better go get changed. Thanks for offering me a ride to school."

"No problem," Tor said with a smile. "I'm going over to the stable to work Top Hat anyway."

Samantha dropped a kiss on Pride's nose, then dashed off across the farm drive to the cottage that she and her father shared. Whitebrook was moderate in size for a breeding and training farm. In addition to the mile training oval, with an inner turf course, there were three stabling barns—one for the horses in training, a smaller stallion barn, and the broodmare and foaling barn. The Reeses' white farmhouse was farther up the drive, and behind the barns was the cottage Len and Charlie Burke, Pride's wizened old trainer, shared. Surrounding it all were acres of white-fenced paddocks.

Forty-five minutes later Tor dropped Samantha off at the doors of Henry Clay High in Lexington. Tor had graduated the June before but was taking a semester off before college so that he and Top Hat, his big white Thoroughbred jumper, could train and prepare for the National Horse Show in New York during the winter.

Tor smiled a farewell as Samantha climbed from the car. "I'll see you this afternoon for your lesson," he said.

"I'll be there," she promised. Although Samantha had galloped horses for years, she'd never tried jumping until Tor had offered her free lessons the spring before. Though she didn't always have time for regular lessons, she was slowly learning. Samantha gave a last wave and hurried inside. Yvonne was already waiting at Samantha's locker, her dark eyes shining as she talked with Maureen O'Brien, the features editor of the school paper.

"I thought you missed the bus or something!" Yvonne called as she caught sight of Samantha.

"I was running late," Samantha said. "Tor gave me a ride in. I thought I told you that he was coming over to watch the workouts this morning."

"Right, I forgot." Yvonne pushed a strand of straight black hair behind her ear. "And how did it go?"

"Pride worked great, like he always does. Sierra . . ." Samantha shook her head and frowned as she quickly spun her locker combination.

11

"I wasn't just talking about the horses," Yvonne teased.

Samantha gave her friend a scowl. Yvonne, with the dark beauty of her part English, part Spanish, part Navajo heritage, had been dating Jay Schneider since the junior prom the spring before. Now she wanted to get Samantha and Tor together—she was convinced Tor liked Samantha as more than a friend. Since Samantha wasn't sure herself what to make of her budding relationship with Tor, she hated it when Yvonne teased her.

"Tor asked Mike about training Sierra for steeplechasing," she said, changing the subject. "Tor thought that racing over fences might keep Sierra more interested."

"Hey, all right!" Yvonne said. Yvonne had been riding with Tor and Samantha one day the previous July when Sierra had jumped the paddock fence and taken a run around the Whitebrook grounds. Samantha, Yvonne, and Tor had been forced to trick Sierra in order to catch him. None of them had forgotten the colt's spectacular jump over the fence. Like Tor, Yvonne felt the colt had potential as a jumper. "What did Mike say?"

"That he didn't know anything about training steeplechasers, and that he wants to keep working Sierra on the flat."

Yvonne made a face. "Darn."

"What's this about steeplechasing?" Maureen asked, her pixielike face alight with interest. "That would be a really good column for you to write, Sammy." Maureen had started Samantha writing monthly columns about the racing industry when they were freshmen. Now that they were juniors and had more say on the newspaper staff, they were thinking of expanding the column.

"It's just an idea we had for Sierra, since he's been training so poorly," Samantha answered. "But it's not anything I can put in a column. I don't know much about it myself."

"Well, you'll have plenty to write about anyway with Pride running in the Breeders' Cup," Maureen told her. "You must be getting excited. I sure wouldn't mind trading places with you!"

"No way," Samantha said with a grin. "I can't wait to see California and the Santa Anita track."

"It's really different from Kentucky," Yvonne put in. "There's the ocean, and the mountains, and palm trees, and smog." Yvonne had grown up in New Mexico and had been to Southern California a number of times. "Too bad you won't have time to see much except the track."

"I know. I'll only be there three days," Samantha said, "but I'm happy enough that Ashleigh and Mr. Townsend are paying my airfare out and back so that I can be with Pride."

"They ought to," Yvonne said. "They know Pride runs his best when you're around."

"If I could only get Sierra to do as well! At least Mike said he doesn't mind if I put in some extra time with him."

"You're not skipping your lesson with Tor this afternoon?" Yvonne exclaimed.

"No, but starting tomorrow, I'm taking Sierra out every day. Mike said this morning that if Sierra doesn't improve, he might have to sell him."

"No!" Yvonne exclaimed. "He can't sell Sierra!"

"Oh yes, he can," Samantha said unhappily. "Sierra's his colt."

2

"HOW COME YOU LOOK SO DOWN?" YVONNE ASKED SA-
mantha that afternoon as they walked the half-mile to
Tor's stable. "Are you that worried about Mike selling Sierra?"

"No. Not yet," Samantha answered. "I still have
time to work with him. Mike's not going to do anything that soon. It's just that I always get a little nervous before my jumping lessons."

"Why?" Yvonne asked in amazement. "I've seen
you gallop half-green, high-strung Thoroughbreds on
the track, and you're *never* nervous."

"This is different. It's stupid, but I feel sort of self-
conscious with Tor watching," Samantha admitted. "I
mean, he's so good. And I'm supposed to be a good
rider, so when I make a mistake, I really feel like a
jerk. Does that make sense?"

"Yeah, I know what you're talking about," Yvonne
said. "When I got Jay to come watch my lesson, I

couldn't do anything right. I think I was trying too hard to impress him. I mean, I'd been going out with him six months and it was the only time I could get him to watch me ride."

"He should have been there to see you win the blue ribbon in intermediate jumping in September," Samantha said. "It's really too bad he's not interested in your riding."

Yvonne shrugged. "There are other things about him I like. He knows a lot about acting, and most of the time he's good to talk to. And he loves to dance," Yvonne added with a grin.

Tor was waiting for them at the stable entrance. He smiled eagerly as they approached. "I've got Cocoa tacked up and ready to go," he said to Samantha. "I've set up a small course. You haven't had much of a chance to practice lately, but I don't think you'll have any problems."

Samantha hadn't had a lesson with Tor in weeks. She'd been too busy getting Pride ready for the Jockey Club Gold Cup that had taken place in early October. "How big are the fences?" she asked uncertainly.

"Oh, five foot or so," Tor answered with a straight face. He laughed when he saw Samantha's expression. "I'm only kidding. The highest is four feet—you won't have any trouble."

Samantha let out a breath of relief. She wasn't anywhere near good enough to jump five feet. "Let me just change into my boots." She sat down on a nearby bench, removed her sneakers, and pulled on the boots she'd brought to school with her. Yvonne asked

Tor about a local show she wanted to enter in November. Several stable horses poked their heads over their stalls, and one of the young grooms walked past with an armful of rubbing cloths used to wipe down a horse after bathing and grooming.

A moment later Tor, Samantha, and Yvonne were heading down the aisle toward the large indoor ring attached to the stable building. Samantha unclipped Cocoa, an experienced bay stable horse, from the crossties where Tor had left him, and they went into the now-empty indoor arena.

Tor had set up six jumps around the huge oval ring. Samantha studied them carefully. There were four pole fences along one side. Samantha knew the series was called gymnastics. A single stride separated each of the fences, and each fence was increasingly higher than the last, beginning with a crossbar and ending with a four-foot horizontal. On the opposite side of the ring were a parallel jump, made up of two closely spaced fences to be jumped as one, and a wide wall, made of plywood painted to look like stone. Samantha knew she'd need a lot of leg going over that one.

"All set?" Tor asked.

"Yup." Samantha adjusted Cocoa's stirrups, then lifted the reins over his head and prepared to mount. Yvonne walked to the small set of bleachers at the end of the ring and took a seat. She would only be watching that afternoon.

After Samantha had warmed up Cocoa at a walk, trot, and canter, circling the ring twice at each pace,

Tor explained the course. "Let's start with the gymnastic. Let me explain, since you haven't done this before. Bring him up to the crossbar at a trot. The rhythm is going to be squeeze, jump, land, squeeze, jump, land—right through the whole series. You've got to get him ready for the next fence as soon as he lands, or he'll refuse."

Samantha nodded.

"After you come through the gymnastic," Tor continued, "circle around the bottom of the ring and jump the parallel. Keep him collected between the fences, or you won't meet the jump right," Tor warned. At Samantha's nod, he added, "After you've done that, I want you to go on and jump the wall."

"But it's too tight an angle between the parallel and the wall!" Samantha said in alarm.

"You're not going to go directly from one to the next," Tor explained. "When you come off the parallel, canter forward to the top of the ring, then circle back and approach the wall from the opposite direction."

Samantha studied the course he described. "That's a lot of fences," she said uncertainly.

Tor smiled up at her. "You can do it!"

Samantha hoped he was right. She wished she felt the same confidence on the jump course that she felt on the training oval. Turning Cocoa, she trotted him up around the top of the ring for their run through the gymnastic. She checked her position in the saddle—head up, shoulders and back straight, heels down, elbows in. Cocoa trotted eagerly toward the crossbar, and they started through the gymnastic.

"Jump . . . land . . . squeeze . . . jump . . ." Samantha squeezed extra hard before the last fence, and she knew she'd gotten the extra height she needed. They landed and started cantering off. Samantha looked ahead to the parallel. She held Cocoa at a collected canter and counted strides as they approached the wider jump. The parallel was only three and a half feet tall, but Cocoa would need to make a strong jump to clear the back-to-back fences. Samantha calculated their approach. At what she felt was the right moment, she gave rein, squeezed hard with her legs, and they soared.

To Samantha's relief, they cleared the jump and landed smoothly. She was already looking ahead, calculating the half-circular angle of their approach to the last fence. She kept Cocoa in a collected canter as she turned him at the top of the ring and pointed him at the wall. He went gamely toward it. Samantha reminded herself that she'd need a lot of leg to get over. *One more stride*, she thought, *then squeeze . . .*

The next thing she knew, Cocoa was skidding to a stiff-legged halt, and Samantha had all she could do to stop herself from flying straight over his head! Only instinct saved her, as she grabbed handfuls of Cocoa's mane and held on tight until she slid back down his neck. She'd lost one of her stirrups. Samantha was thankful that Cocoa was a well-schooled stable horse—he didn't try to bolt off with her as she quickly slipped her foot back into the iron and regathered the reins, but she was embarrassed by her failure.

"What did I do wrong?" she asked with a red face as Tor strode over.

"You asked him to jump too late," he said. "You were a half-stride too close to the jump, and he knew it."

Samantha frowned in thought. "So what do I do? Extend his stride between the jumps, or shorten it?"

"It would be easier to shorten it. After you come off the turn at the top of the ring, collect him a little bit more, tighten up his stride, and he should meet the jump just right."

"Got it," said Samantha, but now she was even more nervous. *Concentrate on each fence one at a time,* she told herself as she and Cocoa set out. *Don't think about the wall until you're riding toward it.*

Cocoa was with her every inch of the way as they bounded through the gymnastic, once again soared over the parallel, and cantered away from it toward the top of the ring. Turning Cocoa, Samantha looked ahead to the wall and collected more rein. She felt Cocoa's strides shorten. His legs seemed to be churning beneath her as they headed toward the wall. *Stride . . . stride . . . stride,* Samantha thought. *Squeeze!* This time Cocoa gave a huge thrust with his hindquarters, and they were in the air, soaring over the jump with many inches to spare. Samantha was so relieved that she relaxed too soon and wobbled badly as her weight bumped back into the saddle. She nearly lost her stirrups again.

"Hey," Tor called, "after a jump like that, don't lose it now!"

Samantha quickly recovered, forcing her heels

down and gripping with her legs. She cantered Cocoa in a circle, then slowed him to a trot as she patted his neck. "It was okay?" she asked Tor breathlessly as she pulled Cocoa down to a walk.

"Great! The best jumping you've done so far."

Yvonne hurried over. "Okay, kiddo! Nice job."

"I wasn't feeling too good after I botched the wall the first time," Samantha admitted.

"You made up for it the second time," Tor told her. "A good way to end your lesson."

Feeling a huge sense of relief at Tor's praise, Samantha dismounted and pulled up the stirrups. Since Tor had another class coming into the ring in a few minutes, she'd walk Cocoa outside in the stable yard. All three of them headed toward the exit, Samantha leading Cocoa.

"Have you thought any more about what you're going to try with Sierra?" Tor asked as he walked along at Samantha's side.

"I thought I'd take him out on the trails tomorrow and give him a change of scene."

"Want some company?" Tor asked.

Samantha's green eyes lit up with surprise. "Sure! But don't you have classes to teach?"

"I have tomorrow afternoon off. I'll pick you up at school."

"That would be great." Samantha had planned on asking her father to ride with her, since she couldn't, for safety's sake, take Sierra out alone. To have Tor along would make the ride all the better. "Do you want to come, too, Yvonne?" she added quickly, not wanting her best friend to feel left out.

"I can't. I told Jay I'd go to drama club rehearsals with him. You know he has a big part in the play they're putting on this winter. Actually, I'd rather go riding with you, but I think he'd get pretty upset if I don't show up." Yvonne shrugged, then smiled. "I'll come over and ride with you on the weekend."

"It's a deal."

Tor picked Samantha up from school the next afternoon. It was a perfect day for a ride. The sky was a cloudless blue, and the air was crisp and filled with the scents of fall.

When they arrived at Whitebrook, Len had Sierra and one of the better exercise ponies tacked up and waiting for them. Charlie Burke, the old trainer who'd helped make champions out of Wonder's Pride and his dam, Ashleigh's Wonder, was standing with Len.

"So you're not ready to give up on him," Charlie said to Samantha. He pushed back his felt hat and studied Sierra, who was prancing at the end of the lead shank Len held.

"No," Samantha said firmly. "I know Mike's pretty disgusted with him, but Sierra's too good a horse to write off. I think he'll settle down and start concentrating."

Charlie pursed his lips. "I admire your determination, but you know not every horse is cut out for the track."

"I know," Samantha said, "but I'm going to try."

"Nice day for a ride, anyway," Charlie said. "Do you know if Ashleigh's coming over this afternoon?"

"She said she'd definitely be here, since she missed Pride's workout yesterday," Samantha told him.

"I want to talk to her about the trip to Santa Anita. Clay Townsend was over earlier and said he's booked Pride on a flight out of Lexington on Friday morning—sooner than I'd expected."

"Pride wasn't supposed to leave until Sunday!" Samantha exclaimed worriedly. "Will Ashleigh be able to leave so soon?"

"That's what I want to find out," Charlie answered. "I'll be traveling with the colt in any case, but it would be better if Ashleigh were along, too. Well," he added, "I've got things to do. Have a good ride."

Samantha frowned. She knew Charlie was thinking of the past summer, when the Townsends had tried to take control of Pride's training schedule away from Ashleigh and Charlie. The resulting tension had been harmful to Pride. Samantha hoped Mr. Townsend wasn't going to repeat his mistake now.

As Charlie headed back into the barn, Samantha and Tor mounted up. Tor's mount, Roman, was a dapple-gray gelding who was frequently used as a pace horse. Although Roman had speed when he needed it, he had an easygoing disposition, which would help balance Sierra's flightiness. They set out from the stable yard and trotted the horses up a grassy lane between the paddocks. Sierra was already showing himself to be a handful. He playfully thrust his head against the reins and eyed Roman as if he would like nothing better than to take a nip out of the gelding's neck.

Yet Samantha could see that the colt was enjoying the trip out over the trails. There was an enthusiastic spring in his step, and his ears were pricked as he gazed out over the paddocks, where mares, yearlings, and weanlings grazed peacefully.

"Did you work with Top Hat this morning?" Samantha asked Tor as they trotted along.

"I school him for at least an hour every day. He pretty much knows everything he has to know, but both of us have to stay at our peak physically. We have another three or four fairly big shows before the National Horse Show."

"You've done well so far," Samantha said admiringly. She had gone to watch Tor and Top Hat compete in a big jump show in Lexington and had been awestruck by Tor's talent.

"Well, we've worked hard enough! I just hope we can both hold together till then."

Samantha understood what Tor meant. He and Top Hat had had a hectic summer and fall, competing in show-jumping events all over the East Coast and continually gaining in the national rankings. Tor had rarely been in Lexington on the weekends. "Do you feel good about the Southern California show?" she asked.

"Yeah. We've already competed against some of the entrants, but you never know. It's too bad you have to fly back Sunday—you won't be able to see us."

"I have to get back for school," Samantha said.

"My father doesn't want me to miss too many days. But I'll be thinking about you. At least on Saturday you'll get to watch the Breeders' Cup races with me."

"I'm looking forward to that!" Tor said, smiling at her.

Samantha's cheeks warmed under his gaze.

"Sierra seems to like it out here," Tor said a moment later. "He's settling down. He's an altogether different horse when he's interested. You know, he's definitely got the conformation to make a jumper. If Mike did sell him, what kind of price could he get?"

"That's not going to happen if I can help it," Samantha said firmly.

"I know. I'm just curious."

Samantha thought it over. "Well, considering his bloodlines and how well Maxwell's other two-year-olds have been doing, maybe a hundred thousand dollars."

"Wow!"

"That's just a guess. If he never makes it to a racetrack, it could be less. This is the spot where he jumped out of the paddock, remember?" Samantha motioned with her head toward the white five-foot-high fence.

Tor chuckled. "I sure do. Boy, he led us around on a chase that day! Which way do you want to go? Should we head up this trail?"

"Yes, let's," Samantha agreed. They turned the horses off the grass lane and started trotting up a wide cleared path that meandered through the ten-acre track of woodland behind Mike's pastures.

"Gorgeous, isn't it?" Samantha said as she gazed at the sun slanting through the brilliantly colored foliage. "And look how well he's behaving."

The next instant Samantha wanted to eat her words. Sierra's head shot up. Suddenly he gathered his muscles, and with a loud snort, he bolted at a full gallop up the trail.

Startled, Samantha tried to gather her wits. She'd been having such a good time that she'd let her guard slip. Now she knew Sierra would take full advantage of it! She leaned back in the saddle, tightened her grip on the reins, and steadily pulled back on them. But in her moment of relaxation, Sierra had grabbed the bit in his teeth. As long as he held the bit, he couldn't feel the pressure from the reins—and he wasn't about to respond to Samantha's voice. He tore up the trail at a breakneck pace. Samantha desperately tried to keep a clear head. If she could sit the ride out, Sierra should eventually drop the pace on his own—she hoped!

The trail ahead was wide, but twisting, and there were still obstacles, like low-hanging branches, to avoid. Sierra's hooves pounded over the soft ground. His huffed breaths echoed in the quiet woodland.

"Whoa, boy . . . whoa!" Samantha called firmly, trying to get through to the galloping colt. "Let's just slow down." But Sierra continued to plunge forward. The reins in Samantha's hands felt like useless ribbons. Behind her, she heard the pounding of Roman's hooves as Tor came in pursuit, but she knew Roman wasn't fast enough to catch Sierra when he was running at full throttle. *If only he would run like this on the track,* Samantha thought.

She ducked to avoid a low-hanging branch, and Sierra took her lowered crouch as a signal to increase his speed even more. *Don't panic!* Samantha told herself desperately. *If you panic, you'll never get him under control.* But she'd never been on a runaway horse before. She thought suddenly of the runaway horse that had killed her mother when it had bolted through the rail of a Florida training track. No! She couldn't think such horrible thoughts! She'd totally lose it if she did, yet Samantha was finding it easier and easier to imagine disaster. What if Sierra fell? What if he injured himself? Mike would have her head!

She tried to look ahead and steer their course, despite their mad pace. They wildly rounded a curve in the trail. Then Samantha saw a fallen tree not a dozen yards ahead, completely blocking their path. It must have fallen in the storm they'd had a few days before, because it hadn't been there the last time Samantha had ridden over the trails.

The tree was huge, with branches thrusting up from its massive trunk. Sierra must have seen the obstacle, but he didn't pause in his headlong flight for even the briefest instant. Samantha hauled on the reins. The leather bit into the flesh of her hands, and her arm muscles ached, but she got no response from Sierra.

What am I going to do? she thought with rising fear. If she couldn't stop Sierra, they'd have to jump. But could they clear the tree? She had an awful vision of

27

Sierra's legs catching in the branches, and the two of them crashing in a tumble of flying limbs and bodies.

Samantha tried to remember everything from her lessons with Tor—but she'd never jumped over anything so big, and certainly not at a gallop! Some of the branches had to reach six feet in the air, and they spread out at least that distance across the path. Each of Sierra's powerful strides was bringing them closer.

Swallowing back her panic, Samantha tried to steady herself in the saddle and to steer the colt toward the least threatening part of the massive trunk, below the point where the branches sprouted upward. Sierra refused to be guided. He headed straight toward the center of the obstacle. Samantha knew she had no choice now but to get him over it. She couldn't let herself think of the consequences if they didn't clear the tree!

She braced herself in her jump seat and tried to judge their distance. *Another two strides*, she thought. She prepared to squeeze hard with her legs and release rein, but when was the perfect moment?

Just as Samantha was sure they would crash headlong into the tangle of wood, Sierra slowed his pace fractionally. She felt him gathering his muscles. Then he was curling his forelegs and thrusting with his powerful hindquarters. An instant later they were soaring.

"Clear it!" Samantha cried in desperation, as if her words could get them over. She was stretched out over the colt's neck with her arms fully extended. Instinctively she forced her heels down as far as they would go in the stirrup irons and grabbed handfuls of Sierra's mane for balance. They seemed to be in the air forever as Sierra stretched himself over the width of the spreading branches.

Then Sierra's front feet connected with the solid dirt of the trail. Samantha slid forward, up on Sierra's neck. In the next instant, Sierra's hindquarters descended and his rear feet hit the ground. Samantha was thrown back with a heavy bounce into the saddle. She lost her stirrups, but Sierra was already bounding off again at a gallop. Samantha's fingers were still entwined in Sierra's mane, but she had only her legs to hold her on the slippery saddle, and she was badly off balance.

Samantha's heart was pounding in her ears as Sierra roared on up the trail. She tried frantically to grip his sides with her legs and retrieve her lost stirrups.

Suddenly the colt turned sharply around a curve. Samantha knew she was going to lose it. Her seat was too insecure. As Sierra galloped to the left, she was pitched headlong to the right. She tried to save herself by clinging to his mane, but her hands seemed to have no strength left. Her fingers slid weakly from the reins, and the next moment she was being somersaulted through the air toward the side of the trail.

3

SAMANTHA LANDED HEAVILY ON HER BACK IN A CLUMP OF thick brambles. She cried out in pain as several thorns ripped through her light jacket and shirt. The canes had broken her fall, but the impact had knocked the wind out of her. For a moment she lay unmoving as she tried to catch her breath.

Tor pounded up and skidded to a stop beside her. His expression was frightened. "Sammy! Are you all right?"

"I'll be fine," Samantha answered, hoping it was true. "Get Sierra. He galloped up the trail."

She could see that Tor didn't want to leave her, but she knew they couldn't let a valuable Thoroughbred run loose—he might seriously injure himself. As Tor galloped off, his blond hair flying, Samantha pulled deep breaths of air into her lungs. Every muscle in her body felt like rubber, and her hands had begun to shake. Slowly she drew her feet under her, leaned on her elbows, and tried to extract herself from the thorns.

By the time she was finally clear of the brambles and standing shakily on the trail, the backs of her hands were covered with bleeding scratches. She knew there were scratches on her face as well, but otherwise, she thought she was okay. She didn't feel any sharp pains, which could mean broken bones. She flexed her knees, testing her legs. They were still wobbly, but everything worked. Now her main worry was Sierra.

Unsteadily, Samantha started up the trail. She rubbed her lower back, which felt sore—she'd need a long soak in a hot tub that night. She heard and saw nothing on the trail. She prayed Tor would catch the colt before there was a worse disaster.

It's my fault, Samantha thought miserably. *I should have been on constant alert!* She knew what Sierra was like and how quickly he could pull a crazy stunt.

The farther she walked, the more frightened she became. There was no sign of Tor and Roman, or Sierra. Straining her ears, she thought she heard noises ahead—the snorted breath of a horse, the snap of a broken twig.

She picked up her pace, even though her muscles protested. As she rounded a curve she saw Tor and Roman approaching. And behind them, being led by his reins, was Sierra!

"You caught him!" she cried in relief.

"I found him in a clearing at the other end of the trail," Tor said. "He'd stopped to have a snack."

"Is he all right?"

"He looks fine," Tor answered. His eyes widened as he got a closer look at Samantha's scratches. "But *you* look terrible!"

"I'll be okay. I'm just a little scratched up." Samantha's eyes were on Sierra. The colt's condition was her main concern. He was tossing his head, and he definitely didn't look any the worse for his mad gallop. Samantha thought he was looking rather proud of himself.

"He does look okay," she said, turning to Tor. "Thank you so much! I don't know what I would have done if you weren't here."

"I was pretty freaked when I saw that tree, especially when I saw that he was going to jump it!" Tor shook his head. "I haven't been that scared in a long time."

"I couldn't stop him." Samantha said. "He had the bit in his teeth. I was terrified. But he cleared it."

"It was an amazing jump!" Tor glanced back at Sierra. "Especially for a horse that's had no training."

"But how did you get Roman over?" Samantha asked in wonder. "He's never jumped."

"Every horse can jump. I didn't even think about it—I just knew I had to get to you and Sierra. I jumped Roman over the lowest part of the tree, though it took some encouragement."

Samantha let out a long breath. "I guess I'm pretty lucky."

"Yeah!" Tor said. "But that was also pretty incredible riding, Sammy."

Samantha looked at him in surprise. "You've got

to be kidding! All I managed to do was stay on—and I couldn't even do that after Sierra jumped."

"But you didn't panic. That's the important thing."

Samantha glanced away from Tor's admiring gaze. She'd panicked, all right, but she decided she wouldn't tell Tor that.

"Do you think you can ride, or would you rather we walk back?" Tor asked.

"I'm fine," Samantha said. "I'll ride. We can go out the other end of the trail. It comes out on one of the lanes."

Tor handed her Sierra's reins, then he quickly got out of Roman's saddle.

"What are you doing?" Samantha asked. "I thought we were going to ride."

"You ride Roman back," Tor answered, "and I'll ride the monster. I think he's gotten rid of his high spirits, but I don't want to chance it."

Samantha didn't have the energy to argue. She handed Sierra's reins to Tor and mounted Roman, who was surprisingly calm for all the excitement. They turned the horses and headed out the other end of the trail.

Samantha noticed Tor throwing worried glances her way. Finally she laughed and said, "Don't look so nervous. I didn't bang my head. I'm not suddenly going to fall out of the saddle."

Tor grinned sheepishly. "Well, that looked like a pretty hard fall."

"It could have been worse," Samantha reminded him.

"That's true. And now we know for sure that Sierra definitely can jump."

Samantha glanced at the unrepentant colt, who was stepping easily along the trail. "But I've got to do what Mike wants and try to turn him into a flat racer."

When they rode into the stable yard, Samantha saw her father standing with Mike near one of the barns. Ashleigh Griffen, Mike's girlfriend and Pride's half-owner, was with them. When they saw Samantha, they all stopped talking and stared.

"What happened?" Samantha's father cried in alarm, hurrying toward her. Samantha knew he'd never gotten over his fear of her having a riding accident like her mother's.

"I'm fine, Dad," she said quickly. "I just took a little tumble."

"On Roman?" Mr. McLean asked in amazement.

"No, on Sierra." As Samantha and Tor dismounted, Samantha explained what had happened, leaving out the more frightening details for her father's sake. "It wasn't Sierra's fault. I wasn't paying close enough attention, and he spooked at something," she said, although she was only guessing at that.

"Are you sure you're all right?" Ashleigh asked, her hazel eyes searching Samantha's face.

"No broken bones," Samantha assured the older girl, who'd been her friend since the McLeans had first moved to Lexington. "Tor's the hero. He caught Sierra after I fell."

"Thanks, Tor," Mike said. "I appreciate it. This colt sure is turning into a handful!"

"Like I said," Samantha put in quickly, "it wasn't his fault."

Len and Charlie had come out of the barn to listen. "Well," Len told Sierra, "looks like you've been up to mischief again."

Sierra thrust his nose in the air and pulled back his lips as if he were laughing. Samantha tried not to laugh herself. No matter how much trouble he caused, Sierra sure had personality.

"We walked back from the trails," Samantha said to Len, "but he still may need some cooling out."

"I'll take care of him." Len shook his head at the colt as he took Sierra's reins and led him off.

"Are you sure you want to put in extra time on him?" Mike asked Samantha as he watched the departing colt. "It could be a waste of effort—and he certainly doesn't seem to appreciate it!"

"I'm sure," Samantha said firmly. Before Mike could say any more, she turned to Ashleigh. "Will you be able to leave with Pride and Charlie on Friday?" she asked.

"I'll manage it. I want to be with Pride. I don't want *anything* to upset him before the Breeders' Cup."

"Neither do I," Samantha said. "We've worked too hard."

A little over two weeks later, on the last Friday in October, Samantha prepared to board her flight to Los Angeles. Her father waited with her until her flight was called. As she rose to go to the gate, he hugged her and kissed her cheek.

"Have a good time, sweetheart!"

"I will, Dad. Keep an eye on Sierra for me while I'm gone."

He laughed. "I don't know what it is between you and that colt—you sure pick some tough ones. We'll be rooting for Pride."

"He'll do a good job," Samantha said. "I know it."

Once on board, Samantha settled into her window seat and thought about the exciting weekend ahead. Ashleigh had called frequently from Santa Anita to let Samantha know how Pride was doing. He'd adjusted well to his new surroundings and had put in two fantastic works for Ashleigh and Charlie. Still, Ashleigh had said that she'd be glad when Samantha arrived. She could see that Pride missed Samantha. And Samantha sure had missed Pride!

Samantha leaned her head against the seat back as the plane climbed into the skies. The next thing she knew, she was awakened by the pilot announcing that they were beginning their approach to Los Angeles International Airport. Samantha sat up quickly. She hadn't meant to fall asleep. She'd wanted to see the country they were flying over, since she'd never been so far west before. Now, as Samantha gazed excitedly out of the window, she saw the blue Pacific Ocean on one side and a range of mountains on the other. Between them the city of Los Angeles was shrouded in a grayish-yellow cloud of smog.

The plane began its descent, and soon they were landing with a quick screech of tires. The plane's engines reversed loudly as they gradually slowed and began to taxi toward the terminal.

Samantha was soon exiting with the other passengers. As she entered the terminal, she searched the crowd for Ashleigh. Almost immediately she spotted the dark-haired young woman, and they both waved and smiled.

"Did you have a good trip?" Ashleigh asked when Samantha reached her side.

"I fell asleep, so I missed all the sights."

"Don't worry," Ashleigh said brightly, "there's plenty to see here. Pride's doing great. The press are driving us crazy. Mr. Townsend got in yesterday—along with Brad and his girlfriend, but fortunately Brad's stayed away from the stables. Oh, guess what? Brad and Lavinia got engaged!"

"You're kidding!" Samantha exclaimed. Brad Townsend, the handsome and arrogant son of the owner of Townsend Acres, had made both Ashleigh's and Samantha's lives miserable with his bossy interference. He was the one who'd nearly ruined Pride's career. "How can she stand him?"

Ashleigh laughed. "Well, we both know that Lavinia is as big a snob as Brad. Maybe she doesn't notice his flaws."

"At least he's staying away from Pride," Samantha said.

"Right. Neither of the Townsends has interfered at all with Charlie and me. It's a nice change from last summer, when they were trying to take over."

"Are things better at Townsend Acres?" Samantha asked.

"Not much better. Pride's purse money helped, but Townsend Acres doesn't have as many horses in training as they did, and money is still tight, from what I hear. I've also heard that Lavinia's got loads of money, so that ought to make Brad happy. Is that all the luggage you have?" Ashleigh asked, motioning at Samantha's canvas bag. When Samantha nodded, Ashleigh started leading her toward one of the exits. "The car's out here. I rented one so Charlie and I could get around."

They stepped out of the terminal into seventy-degree temperatures and a clear sky above. In the distance, Samantha saw waving palm trees. "It's really different from Kentucky!" she said with a smile. "When I left, it was pretty chilly."

As Ashleigh drove away from the airport, Samantha gazed eagerly out the window. Nondescript buildings lined the wide, traffic-clogged roadways. In the distance, Samantha saw towering hillsides covered with scrub.

"Everything's so brown," she said to Ashleigh. "I never thought of California as brown."

"It's the dry season. The hills get green again after the winter rains."

As Ashleigh confidently steered down one of the freeways, Samantha talked about what had been going on at home. "Last week Tor and I drove over to your parents' place to see Wonder and Townsend Princess." Samantha described their visit to the weanling filly, who was Pride's half sister and the second foal of Pride's dam, Ashleigh's Wonder. Wonder had been bred to Baldasar, Princess's sire, and was due to foal again in May.

"Princess is really growing up, isn't she?" Ashleigh said proudly. "I've got big dreams for her. Of course, I've got a while to go. She won't start yearling training until next fall."

"Do you think the Townsends will want her to train at Townsend Acres?" Samantha asked.

"I'm afraid they will, but I'll try to get them to agree to let her train at Whitebrook."

It seemed no time at all before Ashleigh was pulling into the backside parking lot at Santa Anita. "Leave your bag here," she told Samantha. "We'll drop by the motel after you've seen Pride."

Ashleigh led the way through the rows of backside barns alive with activity. Horses were being walked and bathed in the warm sunlight. Grooms bustled about, carrying tack and feed. Since it was early afternoon, the day's races were already in progress.

"We're over here," Ashleigh said. She was pointing to a barn that looked just like the rest except for Charlie sitting in front of one of the stalls. Samantha's heart leaped when she saw that Tor was with him. She hadn't expected Tor to get to the track until the following day. She'd missed him more than she'd expected in the past week since he had left for California. He had phoned her twice to let her know how he and Top Hat were doing.

When Tor saw her, he smiled widely. "You made it!" he called.

"How was your trip?"

"Fine. How come you're here? I didn't expect to see you until tomorrow."

"Top Hat's been schooling so well, I decided to take the afternoon off. Pride's looking good," Tor said, still smiling.

As he spoke, Pride stuck his head out of his stall and gave a delighted whinny to see Samantha.

"Yeah, I finally made it, boy," she said happily as she hurried over to hug the big colt's head. "You *are* looking good," she added as she stood back and let her eyes sweep over his perfectly conformed chestnut body. "I've missed you! Things aren't the same at Whitebrook without you."

Pride nudged her with his velvet nose and Samantha looked around for the tack box, which she knew would contain a bag of carrots. She found the carrots and broke one in pieces for Pride.

"So you and Top Hat are doing okay in the preliminaries," Samantha said eagerly to Tor.

"We are, or I wouldn't be taking an afternoon off. It looks good for Sunday. Charlie was just telling me that Pride's put in some good workouts, too."

"Have you watched any of the other horses in the Classic field work?" she asked Charlie.

"Yup. Ultrasound's looking good. So are Super Value and Count Abdul. There are a couple of foreign horses, and a couple I haven't seen race before."

"How's Pride taking to the track surface?"

"It's firmer than what he's used to," Ashleigh answered, "but he doesn't seem to mind it. The European horses are having more trouble." She paused and smiled. "But that's to our advantage."

"Yes." Samantha sighed. Already she was feeling the start of nervous jitters, thinking about the following day's race.

"How would you two like to see the rest of the track?" Ashleigh asked Samantha and Tor. "I'll give you guys the grand tour."

"I'd love it," Samantha said. "I've only seen it on television."

"Let's go, then."

For the next hour Ashleigh, Samantha, and Tor walked around the backside barns, studying the other horses that would be running in the seven Breeders' Cup races. The horses were the cream of the crop from the United States, Canada, and Europe. As they headed toward the stabling paddock and walking ring, they had to fight their way through the huge crowds drawn to the track by the Breeders' Cup weekend. Then they went to see the track itself, with its dirt and turf courses and sweeping grandstand. Ashleigh, who had ridden to fame as Wonder's and Pride's jockey, was recognized by several reporters.

"Ashleigh," one reporter asked, "as jockey, trainer, and owner, how are you feeling about Wonder's Pride's chances?"

"I'm confident," Ashleigh said.

"Count Abdul had a spitfire workout Thursday," the reporter reminded her. "And he's a West Coast horse who likes this track."

"We've beaten him before," Ashleigh replied.

"Brad Townsend didn't sound so confident when I

talked to him. He's not so sure your colt's past his slump of last summer."

Samantha saw Ashleigh's eyes narrow angrily. She could tell Ashleigh was furious over Brad's comments. "There were reasons for Pride's slump," Ashleigh answered tightly. "He's back on his toes now."

"He's not going in as the favorite."

"No," Ashleigh said, "but I like it that way."

When the reporters left, Samantha turned to Ashleigh. "I can't believe Brad. Why would he start a rumor like that? The Townsends own a half-interest in Pride."

"Spite," Ashleigh said. "Don't forget Brad was the one who was pushing to change our training methods with Pride and to switch jockeys. None of it worked."

"He's spiteful enough that he actually wants Pride to lose tomorrow?" Tor asked.

"No, I really don't think he wants Pride to lose," Ashleigh said. "That would hurt Townsend Acres. Brad just wants to sound like a big shot."

When they returned to the barn area, Samantha and Tor took Pride out for a leisurely walk, then Samantha fed him his dinner and gave him a quick grooming before covering him with a lightweight sheet.

"I don't know about you guys, but I'm starved," Ashleigh said when Samantha stepped out of Pride's stall and bolted the door behind her. "There's a good restaurant Charlie and I have been going to near the track."

"Sounds fine to me," Tor said. "Then I'll have to get back and check on Top Hat."

Samantha nodded her agreement. She was hungry, too, since she'd missed lunch. Charlie rose from the deck chair he'd placed in the shade of the roof overhang. "Guess it's about that time, and we'll have a full day tomorrow."

It was easier to walk than drive to the restaurant, which was already packed with racing fans and others connected with the business. The hostess knew Ashleigh and Charlie and led them all to a table in the corner. Many people looked over as they sat down. Samantha knew the main topic of conversation at the other tables was the Breeders' Cup.

As they were finishing their meal, a woman came over to their table. "I'm sorry to interrupt you," she said, "but I just had to wish you and Wonder's Pride the best for tomorrow. He's been my favorite since he started racing, even when he wasn't doing so well for a while. My husband and I came all the way from New York to see him race tomorrow. We have faith in him."

"Thank you," Ashleigh said with a grateful smile. "We have faith in him, too."

"Well," Charlie huffed as the woman walked away, "looks like the colt's got some loyal fans."

"He deserves it," Samantha said. She had every confidence that Pride would do well, but she couldn't help remembering the devastating disappointment of Pride's defeats over the summer. *That won't happen tomorrow,* she told herself.

PRIDE LOOKED GOOD AS SAMANTHA LED HIM AROUND THE walking ring with the rest of the field for the Breeders' Cup Classic. His head was up, and his ears were pricked alertly. He moved over the grass with a springy step and drew admiring comments from the crowd gathered around the ring.

Samantha saw Tor and Charlie near the saddling boxes. A few yards away she saw the Townsends talking to one of the television newscasters covering the day's races. Although Brad and his blond-haired fiancée, Lavinia, had avoided the barn area, they were definitely not avoiding all the cameras aimed in their direction. Brad was always ready to take credit where none was due.

Samantha ignored them. She laid a reassuring hand on Pride's shoulder and studied the other horses in the field. They were all saddled and waiting for the moment when the jockeys would enter the ring to mount up. Each one of them was in prime condition.

Her eyes went to Super Value, the dark bay English horse who had nosed Pride out in the Belmont. Super Value had lost to Pride in the Jockey Club Gold Cup the month before, but Samantha knew he was still a big threat. She also studied Ultrasound, the light bay son of Triple Crown winner Seattle Slew. He was known for his late, closing kick. He was one of the horses that had beaten Pride over the summer when Pride was running at his worst.

"I know you can beat these guys today," Samantha said softly to Pride. "You're behaving just like you did before the Derby, and you walloped most of them then." But Samantha's stomach was fluttering with nervous excitement, and she knew she'd be a basket case, waiting for the race to begin. The seven Breeders' Cup races drew the best Thoroughbreds from both sides of the Atlantic, and it was the most important race day in the year. If Pride won the Classic, having already won the Kentucky Derby and Preakness and having come in second in the Belmont, there was a good chance he could be named Horse of the Year.

Samantha saw the jockeys approaching the ring. Charlie came over to her and Pride, and a moment later Ashleigh, wearing the green-and-gold silks of Townsend Acres, joined them. "All set?" Charlie asked Ashleigh as he prepared to give her a leg into the saddle. At Ashleigh's nod, he boosted her up, and she settled into the small racing saddle. "Count Abdul's probably going to go right out front on the

45

lead," Charlie told her. "Let him. We don't want Pride getting in a speed duel and burning himself out. The track's real fast, so you can expect a good pace. You'll want to keep your eye on that English horse. He's had some good workouts and probably will be in contention. Ultrasound's going to be coming with his late kick, and there are a couple of others in the field who could pull off a big surprise."

Ashleigh chewed her lip as she concentrated on Charlie's words. "I think if we lay just off the pace, we should have a perfect shot—if nothing goes wrong," she said.

"Keep your eyes open," Charlie replied. "Good luck."

The jockeys were all mounted, and the field was starting to leave the ring. Samantha led Ashleigh and Pride forward. "Pride's going to give it his best today," she said to Ashleigh.

"We're both going to try," Ashleigh answered, giving Samantha a wobbly smile. "I hope we'll end up in the winner's circle."

Samantha rubbed her hand on Pride's velvet nose and turned him over to the waiting escort rider, who would lead the colt and Ashleigh out to the track. Then she hurried over to Tor and Charlie, and they all set out for the grandstand.

Samantha was so tense she had trouble swallowing. Her face must have shown her state of mind, because Tor gave her a reassuring smile. "Pride's going to do great," he told her, "but I know how you feel. I feel the same way before every show."

"I wish I could stay calm," Samantha answered, "but I never can when Pride's running. It's so important that he does well. People haven't forgotten his losing streak, and I couldn't stand to hear him booed by the crowd again."

"That won't happen," Tor said as they took their seats. "He's a different horse now than he was this summer."

The field had reached the starting gate. Samantha kept her eyes on Pride and Ashleigh as they waited their turn to load. The first three horses went in. Pride walked smoothly into the four post. He looked calm, but eager, as the gate attendants led in the rest of the field. The six horse balked and had to be pushed in from behind. Then all ten horses were in the gate.

Samantha sat tensely as she waited for the start. Her eyes were glued to Pride. An instant later, the gate doors flew open.

"They're off!" the track announcer shouted.

Pride shot out with a tremendous bound. Samantha's heart soared. It was a good start! Count Abdul was out fast, too. He and Pride were sprinting away from the rest of the field. Samantha knew Ashleigh would try to get clear of the worst traffic, then would settle Pride in just off the lead.

But a few strides from the gate, Pride stumbled badly. Samantha rose in her seat and gasped in horror as Pride's forelegs curled under him. He nearly went to his knees, almost pitching Ashleigh from the saddle.

"Wonder's Pride has stumbled!" cried the announcer in alarm. "He's nearly unseated his jockey!"

Samantha watched in a daze as the rest of the field surged past and around Pride and Ashleigh. But Pride was recovering! Ashleigh had managed to hang on. A fraction of a second later, Pride was back on all fours and striding out in pursuit of the field that had gained several lengths on him.

"That's it, boy!" Samantha cried. She knew too well that the stumble could have ruined every chance Pride had of winning. He had lost a lot of ground to some of the best horses in the world. "He's trying," she cried out breathlessly. "Boy, is he trying!"

As the field passed the stands, Pride had already moved up to catch the last four horses in the field. Samantha was thrilled by the immense courage Pride was showing. She began to think that he might have a chance after all. She lifted her binoculars as the field moved into the clubhouse turn. Pride was still moving up—on his own. Samantha frowned as she watched. Ashleigh seemed to be trying to hold the big colt back. "I think something may be wrong, Charlie," she said tightly.

"I'm noticing," the old trainer answered, staring through his own binoculars. "There's no need for Ashleigh to hold him on that tight a rein unless she's trying to pull him up. I wonder if he caught himself when he stumbled."

Samantha tried to focus on Pride's legs to see if they were injured. Often in a stumble, a horse's rear feet would clip a foreleg and bruise or gash it. "I can't see him clearly!" she cried in dismay. "There are too many horses in the way."

"Whatever's going on, that colt isn't about to stop," Charlie muttered. "He's practically hauling Ashleigh's arms from their sockets."

"Wonder's Pride is still gaining!" came the announcer's cry. "After that bad stumble, he's made up a dozen lengths! As they start down the backstretch, it's Count Abdul still setting the pace. He has half a length on Charisma in second, then it's Super Value, winner of this year's Belmont Stakes, another half-length back—and here comes Wonder's Pride, moving up into fourth!"

Samantha wanted to cheer Pride on, but Ashleigh still had a choking hold on the reins. Pride was pulling them forward by his own will to win. He was outside of Super Value as they neared the end of the backstretch. Charisma was dropping back, and Super Value and Pride moved up on the leader, Count Abdul.

"He could win it!" Samantha shouted hoarsely.

"Come on, Pride!" Tor cheered.

Then Samantha saw Pride falter. His powerful strides weakened. Ashleigh stood quickly in her stirrups. Pride continued dropping back as the rest of the field swept around him.

"Wonder's Pride is being eased!" the announcer shouted. "It looks like he may have injured himself in that stumble. Super Value has taken the lead . . . Count Abdul fighting back . . ."

But Samantha wasn't listening anymore. Already she was on her feet, pushing to the end of the row. She saw that Pride was limping as Ashleigh dis-

49

mounted in the middle of the track. Track attendants were rushing out to help her and Pride.

Samantha rushed down the staircase to the grandstand exit, with Charlie and Tor right behind her. Her only thought was to get to Pride. From the roar of the crowd around her, she knew the race was over, but she saw many people looking anxiously up the track toward Pride.

Tor grabbed Samantha's hand as they dashed along. Her fears overwhelmed her. Her worst nightmare was that Pride had broken his leg.

Finally they reached the spot where Pride and Ashleigh stood, surrounded by attendants. The veterinary ambulance was coming quickly down the track. Samantha, Tor, and Charlie edged their way past the attendants. Ashleigh's face was ashen, and tears streaked her cheeks. Samantha froze. Her eyes went to Pride. He held his right foreleg off the ground, with only the toe of his hoof touching the dirt. The back of his leg was covered in matted blood beneath a deep gash. Samantha reeled at the sight. She stumbled to Pride's head and took his muzzle in her hands. Despite his pain, he whickered softly to her.

"Oh, Pride," Samantha said, choking on the words.

"I was afraid he'd caught himself in that stumble," Ashleigh whispered. "I tried to pull him up, but he wouldn't let me. When he kept running so strongly, I figured he was okay." She buried her face in her hands. "Oh, God, if only I'd gone with my instincts! Running on that leg can only have made it worse!"

"Missy," Charlie said quickly, "I doubt you could

have pulled him up, no matter what you did. The colt set his mind on winning, and he gave it a darned good try, injury and all. He's got enough heart for that whole field out there." The old trainer, brow furrowed in a deep scowl, went to Pride's side and carefully inspected the injury. He shook his head, and his mouth tightened.

"Do you think he's fractured something?" Samantha asked weakly.

"Too soon to tell," Charlie said. "Here's the vet." He moved out of the way as the track veterinarian hurried over. Pride grunted when the vet's gentle hands touched his leg.

"Easy, boy," Samantha soothed. "We're trying to help you." She had to blink back tears. It was almost unbearable to see her beloved horse hurting so much.

"It may not be as bad as it looks," Tor said from behind her.

Samantha knew he was right, but she couldn't swallow her fears. Ashleigh reached over and squeezed Samantha's hand as they waited for the vet's diagnosis. Clay Townsend hurried up with a worried expression on his face. "How is he?" he asked anxiously. "What happened? Did he grab himself?"

"Looks like it," the vet said. "It's a bad gash, but we can fix that up. I don't think he's severed a major blood vessel, and there doesn't appear to be a break. But there may be other damage."

The vet put a temporary dressing on the wound and secured Pride's leg against further injury. "Let's get him over to the clinic," he said, rising. "We'll clean and stitch that wound and get some X rays."

Ashleigh quickly went to Pride's side and gently removed his saddle. One of the attendants produced a blanket, which he threw over Pride's back. The colt's beautiful chestnut coat was dark with sweat, and Samantha knew there was the danger of him getting chilled, and also of his going into shock.

The ramp to the ambulance was already down. Samantha slowly led Pride inside. He hobbled up the ramp on three legs.

They all waited outside the vet's examining room for his final diagnosis. Samantha sat with her hands balled into fists. Tor waited beside her, and Charlie and Ashleigh hunched uneasily on chairs opposite. Clay Townsend paced the floor. Brad hadn't shown his face, for which Samantha was grateful. She didn't think she could stand having Brad around when she was already so upset.

"It's a shame," Mr. Townsend said grimly, "but it's just one of those freak accidents. We can only hope this doesn't end up being a career-ending injury." He shook his head sadly. "I thought he was going to win it—and he would have."

"Give him credit for having a load of courage," Charlie said.

"Oh, I do," Townsend answered.

As upset as Samantha was, she couldn't help wondering at the change in Clay Townsend's attitude. A few months before, all he had seemed to think about was money. Now there was only genuine concern for Pride's well-being in his tone and expression.

The door at the end of the waiting room swung open, and the vet walked out. He was still wearing a blood-spattered green gown. "Well, it could be a lot worse," he said. "He put a lot of stress on the leg, running after the injury."

Ashleigh groaned, and Samantha gave her a sympathetic look. "It's not your fault," she said.

"He rapped himself pretty good," the vet continued. "The cut was deeper than it first appeared, but we've cleaned it and stitched him up. It's obviously going to take some time to heal."

"And the X rays?" Mr. Townsend asked uneasily.

"No breaks, although I did spot a bone chip at the joint, which could bother him later. It should be removed."

"Go ahead," Townsend said quickly, then stopped and turned to Ashleigh. "I'm sorry, Ashleigh," he added. "You have something to say about this, too."

Samantha didn't know whether to feel relieved that Pride's injuries weren't worse or upset that the colt would be put through more stress.

"How serious is it to remove the chip?" Ashleigh asked.

"A fairly simple procedure," the vet answered, "and we already have the colt sedated."

"Then, yes, go ahead," Ashleigh told him.

Clay Townsend asked the question that was on everyone's mind. "Do you think he'll ever be able to race again?"

The vet shrugged. "I can't tell you that for sure. It'll be months before he can fully use the leg again.

Just be thankful that his injury isn't life-threatening."

"We are," Samantha said with feeling.

"I'll go ahead and operate," the vet said. "I'll keep him here for a few days, then I think he can be moved to an excellent equine clinic a few miles from here. Until his leg stabilizes, though, I wouldn't advise bringing him back to Kentucky."

As they left the veterinary hospital, they were mobbed by reporters, and all of the reporters' questions were filled with worry and concern. Mr. Townsend answered them. Ashleigh still looked stunned and Charlie grim. All Samantha could think of was that she'd have to leave Pride behind when she flew home the following day. Somehow before then, she'd find a way to see him and comfort him. She discovered her eyes were filling with hot tears. Tor reached for her hand and held it tightly.

SAMANTHA GOT IN TO SEE PRIDE LATE THE FOLLOWING morning. The vet hadn't wanted the colt disturbed before then. She felt tears sting her eyes when she saw her beloved horse. He seemed listless and unhappy, even though the hospital was obviously doing everything to see to his comfort. The stall was roomy, with thick bedding, though Pride was in crossties to prevent him from moving too much. His injured leg was encased in bandages.

"Oh, Pride," Samantha called softly as she reached the stall. "How are you, big guy? Not too good, huh?"

Pride was definitely glad to see her. He nickered to her and thrust his nose forward against her hand as she gently caressed him, but his normally bright eyes were dull, and his head hung.

The vet had walked up behind her. "Don't worry," he said. "He came out of the surgery fine, but he's been through a lot. It'll be a day or two before he starts picking up again."

"Are you sure?" Samantha asked worriedly. "I have to go back to Kentucky today. It's so hard to leave when he's like this."

"I understand," the vet told her sympathetically. "But I promise you he'll get the best care. I never thought I'd have the Kentucky Derby and Preakness winner in my hospital. If anything, I think my staff will spoil him rotten."

Samantha smiled. "I've spoiled him, too."

"I have to go check on my other patients," the vet said. "Stay as long as you like."

Samantha nodded as she continued to stroke Pride's head, but she couldn't stay much longer. Soon Ashleigh would be taking her to the airport. Ashleigh and Charlie were going to stay on with Pride, and she knew they would give him all the attention they could. But she hated having to leave him! She had expected such a wonderful weekend, but instead of Pride ending up in the winner's circle, he'd ended up with an injury that might finish his career.

"The important thing is that you're going to be all right," Samantha said softly to the colt. "You may never race again, but that's okay. We all still love you."

Samantha stayed with Pride until Ashleigh came to pick her up. Since Pride could have only one visitor at a time, they'd all agreed that Samantha should be the first to see him.

"How does he look?" Ashleigh asked anxiously.

"Not very good," Samantha admitted, "but the vet

said he'll pick up in a couple of days. I wish I didn't have to go home!"

"I know," Ashleigh said sadly, "but Charlie and I will be here. I can only stay another few days or I'll miss too many classes, but Charlie will stay here as long as Pride does. Tor's waiting outside to say good-bye to you," Ashleigh added. "He and Top Hat will be competing in a little while, but he said he had a few minutes before he had to be at the show arena."

When they stepped out into the bright sunshine, Samantha saw Tor standing by Ashleigh's rental car. He came over to Samantha and put his arm around her shoulders. "It's rotten that you have to go back so soon, Sammy. But Pride's going to be okay."

"I know," Samantha said. She bit her lip to keep it from trembling. "I hope you and Top Hat do great this afternoon."

"We'll give it our best," Tor said. "You'll get back too late for me to talk to you tonight, but I'll leave a message with your father and let you know how we did."

Samantha managed a weak smile. "Thanks."

"I'll be back in a few days, and I'll come over and see how you're doing with Sierra," Tor added.

In her worry over Pride, Samantha hadn't thought much about Sierra, but she knew that working with the devilish colt would help keep her thoughts occupied while Pride was recuperating.

"We'd better go," Ashleigh said, glancing at her watch.

Tor gave Samantha's shoulders a squeeze. She was

57

in such an emotional daze that his affectionate gesture barely registered. "See you in a few days," he said.

"Thanks for coming over, Tor. And good luck this afternoon!"

Samantha was exhausted when her father picked her up at the airport that night. With the time difference, it was after nine in Kentucky. She hadn't slept well the night before, worrying about Pride, and she hadn't slept on the plane.

Her father gave her a comforting hug as he met her. "I'm sorry about Pride, sweetheart. Everyone at Whitebrook is upset. It must have been awful for you."

"It has been, Dad. The vet says he's going to be all right eventually, but he may never race again."

"It's really too soon to tell, Sammy," her father said reassuringly. "I've seen horses make amazing recoveries, even after injuries worse than his."

"I know," Samantha said. "I should try to look at the bright side. Did Tor call?"

"He sure did," Mr. McLean said in a lighter tone. "He and Top Hat won their division."

"All right! I'm so glad!"

"He said to say hello and that he'll call you tomorrow before he and his father leave California. And Yvonne called," Mr. McLean added. "She saw the race on TV and was very upset. She was afraid Pride had broken his leg, but when she called today, I told her that his injuries weren't that serious, thank heavens."

"I guess I'd better call her tonight, even though it'll

be late when we get home. How's Sierra?"

"As full of mischief as ever. No one's worked him, but Len's been walking him. He's afraid to leave him out in the paddock for fear he'll jump the fence."

Samantha thought of the willful colt, imagining his antics, and felt a little better.

When she got home, Samantha called Yvonne and reassured her about Pride's condition. Yvonne was still upset.

"It was awful to watch," she said. "One minute he's flying down the stretch and the next—"

"I know," Samantha said, remembering her own horror.

Samantha spent the next few days trying to concentrate on Sierra in order to keep her mind off Pride's injury. Yvonne usually came over to Whitebrook to watch. One afternoon, Sierra tried running out with Samantha toward the outside rail. Samantha quickly got him in hand. Since he'd run off with her in the woods, she never allowed him any slack rein, but she had a pretty good idea that Sierra had intended jumping right out of the oval.

She rode off the track, shaking her head.

"Not good, is it?" Yvonne asked sadly.

"Worse than that," Samantha answered. "It's terrible, and I'm not helping. I can't concentrate the way I should—I keep wondering how Pride's doing."

"He's going to be okay," Yvonne said. "You told me Ashleigh said on the phone that the vet's happy with his progress."

"I know. I've got to buckle down. My father and Mike need me to help with the morning workouts this week, too."

"Tor will be back in a couple of days," Yvonne said. "Maybe he can help you with Sierra."

"He can't help with flat training," Samantha answered. But she was looking forward to Tor's return. In fact, she couldn't wait to see him.

Samantha wasn't the only one who missed Pride. The barn cats did too, especially Sidney. Samantha saw him sitting on the partition of Pride's empty stall, looking forlorn.

"I miss him too, Sid," she said, stroking the cat's white-and-black fur. "He'll be back soon. We have to be patient."

On Saturday Tor returned from California. He came over to Whitebrook that afternoon. Samantha was thrilled when she saw his car coming down the drive. His smile was wide and happy as he parked and walked across the drive to meet her.

"You're finally back!" Samantha cried.

"Yeah. It seems like the trip took forever, but we're home!"

"Congratulations on your win. I'm so happy for you!"

"Thanks," Tor said. "I'm pretty happy myself. So how are you doing? What have you heard about Pride?" he asked quickly.

"Ashleigh says Pride's getting better every day. They're moving him to the clinic tomorrow. Otherwise . . ." Samantha shrugged. "It hasn't been great."

"What's wrong? Have you been working with Sierra?"

"Trying to," Samantha said glumly. "We haven't made any progress, and I'm just as much to blame as he is. My heart hasn't been in it. But if Mike sees how badly Sierra's doing, I know he's really going to give up."

"Hey," Tor said with concern, "you've just had a lot on your mind. It can't be as bad as you think. Why don't you try working him this afternoon while I'm here?"

"Well, I could," Samantha said, feeling her spirits lift at Tor's enthusiasm. "Let me tack him up."

Len had walked Sierra that morning, but the colt was still eager to get out of his stall. He tried rushing into the aisle before Samantha even had the lead shank clipped on. "Just wait a minute," she told him as she grabbed his halter. "You'll get out soon enough, but you'd better improve over your last few works."

Sierra eyed her and snorted, but he waited until she had the shank clipped on. Then he strained forward again. Tor took hold of the other side of his halter, and together they clipped him in crossties so that they could tack him up.

"He's full of energy, isn't he?" Tor said with a smile.

"It would be nice if he'd put it to good use for a change," Samantha answered sourly as she buckled the saddle girth and dropped the flap in place. "Okay, Sierra, let's go."

The colt didn't need any encouragement to leave

the barn. He tossed his head eagerly as they stepped out into the weak November sunlight. The weather had stayed comparatively warm for late fall, though Samantha knew it wouldn't last. Tor held the prancing colt as Samantha got into the saddle.

"Don't expect to see too much," she told Tor. But for the first time in days, she was able to concentrate as she rode Sierra onto the track. The colt must have sensed her added determination because he didn't try bucking her off. As Samantha finished lapping the oval at a canter, she saw Tor motioning to her to pull up at the rail.

"Have you tried working him on the turf course?" Tor asked, his eyes bright with inspiration.

Samantha frowned thoughtfully. "I haven't, but it's a good idea. Maybe he'll like the surface better. Mike won't mind—the grass is still in good shape. Come on, let's do it."

Tor followed Samantha as she headed Sierra across the dirt track and stopped at the opening to the inner turf course. Tor slid aside a section of movable fence, then put it back in place when Samantha and Sierra were through. The inner turf course was surrounded by a hedge dividing it from the outer dirt track. Otherwise, it looked much the same, except that the surface was grass, not dirt.

Sierra's head was up, and he pricked his ears as he looked around. "Well, at least we've got your interest," Samantha said as she trotted him up over the grass. She let him become comfortable with the new surroundings before asking him to canter. He moved out strongly. He was listening to her, but Samantha didn't allow herself to become too encouraged. Things could still fall apart. As they finished lapping the oval, Samantha crouched over Sierra's withers and gave him rein. He leaped out into a strong gallop—but he always did that initially, Samantha reminded herself. Would he keep going? Or would he fall off the pace halfway through the workout?

She concentrated on the colt's strides, trying to determine whether he was getting a good grip on the grass surface. To her delight, she could feel that he was. He seemed to be handling the grass better than the dirt. They whipped along the backstretch at a strong, working gallop. Samantha urged him on with her voice. "That's it, Sierra! Keep it up!"

She was amazed to see that Sierra's ears were back. He was actually listening! Had they found the magic trick? Was he a grass horse instead of a dirt horse? Samantha felt her spirits soar as Sierra kept pouring it on into the far turn. They weren't going at breezing speed, but she'd never been able to keep Sierra galloping strongly this long before.

"Come on . . . come on . . . just a little longer!" she cried as they came off the turn. Ahead was the three-quarter-mile marker pole. Tor was standing opposite along the hedge.

We're going to do it! Samantha thought excitedly. For the first time Sierra was concentrating through an entire workout. He hadn't dropped the bit. She could hardly believe it!

A few yards from the marker pole, Sierra pricked his

ears. *Oh, no*, Samantha thought, but they were only two strides from the marker pole, and Sierra swept past it before he dropped the bit and started to slack off.

Samantha stood in the stirrups and pulled Sierra back into a canter. She had intended to end the workout there anyway, and she wouldn't allow herself to be discouraged that Sierra had slacked off in the last strides. She'd kept him going and interested longer than she ever had before.

She couldn't stop smiling as she rode back to Tor. He was grinning, too. "What do you think?" he asked.

"It's the best work he's ever given me," Samantha answered.

"You think running him on the grass is the answer?"

"It's a start!" Samantha said. "I don't want to get my hopes up too high, but I feel a lot better than I did an hour ago."

"You know," Tor said almost wistfully, "I was really starting to think of him as a jumper—even if that's not what Mike wanted. I started doing a little research on training steeplechasers before I went to California."

"You did? Why didn't you tell me?"

"I figured you had enough on your mind," Tor said. "Anyway, it doesn't look like you'll need it now."

"I hope not, because I don't know if I could convince Mike to let us train him as a steeplechaser." Samantha patted Sierra's neck. "Okay, Sierra! You ran like you were supposed to today. We may make a good flat racer out of you yet!"

SIERRA WENT BEAUTIFULLY THROUGH SEVERAL AFTERNOON workouts. Samantha was thrilled, and so was Len when he came out to watch. Len happily spread the word that the colt was finally coming along. If Sierra continued improving as he was, Samantha knew there would still be time to get him ready for the winter races.

"When are you going to have Mike come and watch?" Yvonne asked as they sat down at one of the few empty tables in the crowded cafeteria on Wednesday.

"I want to get in a few more works—so Sierra's really sharp," Samantha said, unwrapping her sandwich.

"But you really think running on the turf has made a difference for Sierra?"

Samantha nodded happily as Maureen came hurrying up and slid her own tray onto their table. "Sammy, I read your article on the Breeders' Cup last night. It must have been hard for you to write about Pride getting hurt, but the article is great! It really grabs you! I was crying at the end."

"Thanks, Maureen," Samantha answered. "I was crying when I wrote it."

"How *is* Pride?" Maureen asked.

"Improving. Ashleigh came home last week, since she couldn't miss any more classes, but Charlie's with Pride, and he calls nearly every day to let us know how Pride's doing."

"It would be awful if he couldn't race again," Maureen said.

"Yeah," Samantha said, "but at least he's healing quickly." And now that Sierra was improving, Samantha had something to keep her busy, so she wasn't constantly worrying about Pride.

"Before I forget to ask," Yvonne said to Maureen, "did you understand that algebra assignment Mr. Clauson gave us?"

"Yup. Do you need help?" Maureen asked between mouthfuls.

"Desperately!" Yvonne said. "I'm totally lost."

"How about in sixth-period study hall?" Maureen offered. "Hey, where's Jay? He usually sits with you."

"He's practicing lines with one of the other guys in the cast for their next play."

"He's really into it, isn't he?" Maureen said.

Yvonne wrinkled her nose. "He sure is. They've got rehearsals after school, too. I was going to invite myself over to Whitebrook this afternoon, Sammy, and watch you work Sierra. Is that okay?"

"Sure!" Samantha said. "You can see how much he's improved."

Just after Thanksgiving, when Samantha's hopes for Sierra were at their highest, Sierra lost interest. He started pulling all his old tricks, and there was nothing she could do to keep him going. Worse, Mike showed up to watch their afternoon work.

"I thought he was improving," Mike said. "It didn't look like it today."

Samantha bit back her frustration and disappointment. "He *has* been improving. He really took to the turf course. But now . . ." She let the sentence hang, unsure of how to explain without making Sierra sound like a complete waste of time. "I'll keep at it," she added quickly.

Mike shook his head. "There's really no point this late in the year, Sammy. We're starting to get freezing temperatures, and pretty soon the turf course will be getting too hard to use. I'm going to take him out of training."

"But I don't mind working with him!" Samantha exclaimed.

"Honestly, I can't see that it's worth it, Sammy. We've already tried everything. It just doesn't look like he *wants* to race. I've always been prepared for that. You win some, you lose some. I'll be heading down to Florida right after Christmas. I've got some really promising horses to take down to Gulfstream."

Samantha felt sick at his words. "You're not thinking of selling him, are you?"

"I can't see much reason not to, but I don't have time now to make any long-range decisions. We'll keep him here over the winter, anyway, and I'll decide what to do with him when I get back from Florida in early spring. Thanks for trying, Sammy." Mike gave her a smile and headed off toward the training barn.

Samantha stared after him with a sinking heart. Mike didn't seem to realize how devastated she was at his decision. She felt numb as she dismounted. Sierra, of course, didn't understand. He mischievously tried to snatch at Samantha's arm with his teeth, but she tightened her hold on the base of his reins and stopped him. "You're in enough trouble," she told him with a scowl. "You don't need to bite me on top of it!"

Samantha was still scowling as she led Sierra toward the stable. What was she going to do? She refused to give up on Sierra, and she definitely didn't want him sold off the farm! There was Tor's idea of turning him into a steeplechaser, but Samantha had always been sure she'd eventually succeed in getting Sierra to perform on the flat. She'd thought of Tor's suggestion as a last resort. She sighed. Maybe they were at the point of last resorts. But none of them knew anything about training a steeplechaser. Samantha didn't even know where to begin!

Len was waiting at the stable entrance when Samantha led Sierra up. "You don't look too happy," he said. "Did he throw in another dud?"

"Not only that," Samantha told him. "Mike was

watching. He's taking him out of training. He's pretty much given up on Sierra."

Len shook his head and laid a weathered hand on Sierra's neck. "You do know how to get yourself in trouble, fella. I don't know what we're going to do with you."

Sierra snorted and tossed his head.

"Too bad you don't understand the mess you're in," Len told the colt. Len rubbed his chin thoughtfully. "What about your friend's idea of turning him into a jumper?" he asked Samantha. "I don't know anything about jump racing, but Sierra knows all the basics of running on the oval. Maybe having a few fences to jump would wake him up."

"I was just going to call Tor," Samantha said. "The problem is, I don't know anything about training a steeplechaser. I don't know if Mike would agree, anyway. He wasn't interested at all when Tor mentioned it before."

"Well, it would be a shame to see this guy sold off the farm. I'd sure miss him."

"So would I! We'll think of something," Samantha said.

Len led Sierra off, and Samantha strode across the drive to the cottage. It was just four o'clock and already growing dark. Tor would be teaching in the indoor ring now. She might be able to catch him between classes.

Once in the kitchen, she dialed his number. One of the stable grooms answered and called Tor to the phone.

"I know you can't talk long, Tor," Samantha said a little breathlessly, "but I thought you'd want to hear what happened." Quickly she told him of Mike's decision.

"So you can try turning him into a steeplechaser," Tor said with excitement.

"But I don't know anything about steeplechasing!" Samantha protested. "I'm not that good at jumping myself yet. And where would I train him? With winter coming, we can't use the turf track here, and there aren't any fences. And Mike would have to approve—and I don't know if he would."

"I'd help you," Tor said quickly. "I'll call a couple of people I know and see if I can get some information, and you wouldn't need to work him outside. There's the riding ring here."

"It's too small."

Tor laughed. "Think positive, Sammy!"

Samantha tried to follow his advice, but it was hard to think positively when there were so many uncertainties. Even if they learned the particulars of training a steeplechaser, and Mike allowed them to train Sierra, Sierra might not like it any better than the flat.

"I'll talk to you later," Tor said. "My class is starting. But this is going to be fun."

Samantha hoped he was right. She was feeling pretty down in the dumps. Pride was still in California and might never race again. And now Sierra was out of training.

Her father came into the kitchen. "I overheard what you said about Sierra. I'm sorry, Sammy, but you have to understand where Mike's coming from."

"Oh, I do," Samantha said with a sigh. "I know Mike can't afford to keep unprofitable horses. It's just that I had all these hopes for him."

"Don't give up." Her father laid a hand on her shoulder. "Mike isn't getting rid of the colt yet, and Sierra might mature over the winter. How about an early dinner? I thought I'd whip up one of my super-duper omelets."

Samantha grinned. "Sure, Dad." Her father wasn't the best cook in the world, but he did make a great omelet.

As Samantha was clearing up the dishes after they'd eaten, there was a knock on the front door. Her father answered it.

"Well, hi, Ashleigh," he said cheerfully. "What brings you over so late?"

"Good news!" Ashleigh told him as she came inside.

Samantha turned eagerly from the table. "About Pride?"

Ashleigh grinned. "Yup. He's coming home to-morrow! Charlie just called me. He's booked a flight for both of them. The vet's given the okay."

"Wonderful!" Samantha cried. She felt like dancing.

"Pride still has to take it easy for a long time, and his leg will need care," Ashleigh explained, "but we can see to that, and he'll be home again."

"It'll be good having the colt back," Mr. McLean said.

"Did you talk to Mr. Townsend?" Samantha asked. "Who's picking Pride up at the airport?"

71

"I talked to him, and I'll pick up Pride and Charlie early in the afternoon. Mr. Townsend said he'd meet us back here. He sounded just as relieved as us that Pride's coming back."

Ashleigh stayed for a few minutes longer. Samantha considered telling her about Mike taking Sierra out of training—maybe Ashleigh could talk to Mike and get him to change his mind. In the end, Samantha decided not to say anything. It wasn't fair to ask Ashleigh to interfere.

After Ashleigh left, Samantha called Yvonne to tell her the news. Yvonne was upset to hear about Sierra, but she gave a shout of excitement when Samantha told her Pride was coming home. "Can I come to Whitebrook with you after school to see him?"

Samantha laughed. "Of course you can, silly. I was going to ask you anyway."

"I'll see if I can borrow my mother's car for the afternoon," Yvonne said eagerly. Yvonne had turned sixteen that summer and had just gotten her license. Samantha's sixteenth birthday was two weeks away. She hadn't had time to start learning to drive yet, but she was hoping to get her own license by late spring.

"Do you think I can trust your driving?" Samantha teased.

"What do you mean? I got the best score in my driving class!" Yvonne protested.

"Just kidding."

Tor called her later, and Samantha told him the news.

"I'll come by after my last riding class—if it's okay," he said.

"Great," Samantha told him.

"I talked to some of my show-jumping friends tonight," he added. "They'll see if they can put me in touch with people who know something about steeplechasing. Keep your fingers crossed."

"I will," Samantha said.

Yvonne's driving made Samantha cringe only once on the way to Whitebrook the next afternoon. Yvonne was so busy talking, she nearly ran a stop sign. But in the end, they arrived safely at the farm. The van that had brought Pride home was parked in the drive beside Clay Townsend's Jeep Cherokee.

Samantha and Yvonne jumped from the car and raced into the stable building. Ashleigh, Charlie, Mike, Len, Mr. McLean, and Mr. Townsend were standing outside Pride's stall. Samantha noticed with relief that there was no sign of Brad. The stable cats were all there, too, welcoming Pride home. Sidney was perched on the stall partition, looking very pleased. His mother, the big-footed tiger, Snowshoe, and his father, the stocky black-and-white tom, Jeeves, were in the aisle rubbing against Len's legs.

Samantha barely paused to greet the others before unlatching the stall door and going in to see Pride. He gave a nicker of absolute delight when he saw her. As she walked over and gently wrapped her arms around his neck, he huffed out sweet breaths and turned to touch his nose to her shoulder.

"Oh, Pride, I'm so glad to see you!" Samantha cried in a choked voice. "I'm so glad you're home! Let me look at you."

Samantha stepped back slightly and gazed at the big colt. His leg was bandaged from knee to ankle, but otherwise he looked fit. His coat shone, and his eyes, which had looked so dull and listless in the hospital, now sparkled with alertness.

"You're looking good, boy, even if your leg's still bandaged. We're going to take good care of you!"

"We sure are," Ashleigh said, coming to the stall door to stand beside Yvonne. "Charlie said he traveled well. It's so wonderful to see him back in his stall here!"

"And feeling so much better," Clay Townsend added. "We'll have our vet look him over, of course. What did they tell you in California before you left, Charlie?"

"The cut on his leg is healing nicely," the old trainer answered. "They took X rays the day before, and his ankle looks good. He can put weight on the leg, but obviously you don't want him to put too much stress on it. The vet recommended moderate exercise this week—walk him up and down the aisle or out on the grass—change the dressing daily and give the leg an ice bath. I'll take care of all that. It'll give me something to do, and I don't think a massage every morning will hurt him, either. But he's going to get bored spending so much time in his stall."

"I'll be with him as much as I can," Samantha said quickly.

"That'll help," Charlie said.

"What did the vet say about the long-term?" Mr. Townsend asked.

"Well, we gradually increase the amount of exercise he gets, though that won't be easy with winter coming. Some horses heal faster than others, but if all else goes well, he may be ready for light exercise under tack in the spring—maybe not, though."

"And there's no guarantee he'll run like he did in the past," Townsend added sadly.

"Nope," Charlie said. "None at all. We'll just have to see."

But for Samantha, having Pride home was all that mattered at the moment. She would lavish him with attention and take each day as it came.

Gradually the others left. Yvonne stayed for a while longer.

"He does look good, Sammy," Yvonne said. "Somehow I was expecting him to look really sick, but he doesn't."

"No, he doesn't," Samantha said with a smile. "And I don't think he'll be too lonely, even when Charlie and I aren't here." She motioned with her head to Sidney, who was sleeping peacefully curled up on Pride's back as the colt chomped on his hay. Snowshoe and Jeeves had taken seats on the stall partition and were busy grooming themselves.

Yvonne grinned. "It's like they're guarding him."

"Maybe they are," Samantha said.

Tor didn't show up until after Yvonne had left. It was already dark, and Samantha was thinking of heading to the cottage. Pride would need to get some rest after his long trip.

"Sorry I'm so late," Tor said as he hurried into the

stable, "but one of my students wanted some extra coaching. Welcome home, fella," he said to Pride as he looked in over the stall door. "It's good to see you back! You must be feeling relieved," Tor added, with a bright smile to Samantha.

"Am I ever! But I think it's time Pride got a little rest. It's been a long day for him." Samantha checked to see that the sheet covering Pride's back was buckled securely. Sidney opened one eye to look at her, then contentedly went back to sleep. Samantha took Pride's muzzle in her hands and dropped a kiss on his nose. "See you later, boy. I'll stop by to check on you after dinner." She let herself out of the stall and said to Tor, "We could go visit Sierra for a minute."

"I'd like to. I've been thinking about him all afternoon. I was wondering," Tor said a little hesitantly, "do you think Mike would mind if I tried him out myself? I know Mike's busy now, and it's a lot to ask, but I can get a better feel for Sierra's movements if I ride him myself."

"Well, I could ask Mike," Samantha said, feeling pleased that Tor was taking such an interest. "The turf course is still usable for a while, anyway. And Sierra sure isn't going to be doing anything else. I'll ask Mike tomorrow and let you know what he says."

The next morning when Samantha approached Mike, she wondered if it was the right time to ask him anything. He was completely frazzled. "Wellspring's come up lame," he told her. "I think he's bucked a shin. This *would* happen just when I've got his schedule set for the winter races!"

"I'm sorry," Samantha said quickly, "but you still have a month before you go south. He could bounce back by then." She hesitated, then plunged on quickly. "Tor was wondering if you'd mind if he tried Sierra out on the turf course."

Mike looked surprised by her question, then he shrugged. "Sure, as long as he takes it easy. I know he's a good rider, and Sierra could always use the exercise." He paused and frowned, then added with a touch of excitement, "Tor's not interested in buying him, is he?"

Samantha frowned herself at Mike's excited tone. "He just wants to try him out," she answered.

"Well, go ahead," Mike said. "I've got to call the vet and have him take a look at Wellspring." He hurried off.

Samantha didn't talk to Tor until that afternoon, when she went to the riding stable for a lesson. "Great!" he said with twinkling eyes. "But I can't get over until the weekend."

"That's okay," Samantha said. "Let's just hope the weather holds out and the turf course isn't a mess. What upsets me is that Mike was hoping you wanted to buy Sierra."

"I couldn't afford him. Don't worry, Sammy," Tor added, "we'll turn Sierra around so that Mike won't even *think* of selling him."

Despite her doubts, Samantha was catching Tor's enthusiasm. Could they actually make a steeplechaser out of Sierra?

AT SCHOOL TWO DAYS LATER, SAMANTHA NOTICED THAT Yvonne was acting strangely. Instead of giving Samantha a cheerful smile and chattering away like crazy, Yvonne barely said a word when they met at Samantha's locker. She looked totally down in the dumps.

"What's wrong?" Samantha asked worriedly. "Are you sick?"

Yvonne shook her head. "I'm fine."

"No, you're not," Samantha said. "I know you too well. Something's wrong."

Yvonne sighed heavily. "Oh, it's Jay. I asked him to come watch me in the stable show next week. It's the last one of the season. He told me he didn't want to sit around and watch a bunch of horses jump over fences. He said he can't understand why I waste so much time at the stables." Yvonne looked ready to cry. "But I love riding! He talks about acting all the time, and I don't get on his case. What's so dumb about my liking horses?"

"Nothing," Samantha said firmly. "But this is kind of what I was afraid of."

Yvonne looked up. "What do you mean?"

"Well, maybe you guys don't like enough of the same things. I mean, he doesn't have any interest in riding, and you're not that crazy about drama."

"So what should I do?" Yvonne asked miserably.

"Be yourself and do what you've always done," Samantha told her. "You're not going to stop riding just because Jay isn't interested, are you?"

"No," Yvonne said. "But he makes me feel like I'm weird because I like riding so much."

"You're not weird! A lot of people don't understand how we can be so wrapped up in horses. But that's their problem. Did Jay ask you to the Christmas dance?"

"Yes."

"Are you going?" Samantha asked.

"I guess," Yvonne said. "I still like him. And I want to go to the dance. I was talking to Tracy, who's on the committee, and she said they've got a super band and neat decorations." Yvonne brightened a little. "Are you going to ask Tor?"

Samantha had been trying to screw up the courage to ask Tor to the dance. Tor had asked her to his prom the spring before, but Samantha hadn't been able to go because Pride was running in the Belmont the same day. Since then, Tor hadn't asked her out again. But he'd hardly ever been home on a weekend—he'd been competing in shows. And Samantha couldn't go out during the week since she had to be up so early to work the horses. When they were together, though, they got along wonderfully. "I'm thinking about it," she told Yvonne.

"Well, do it!" Yvonne said emphatically. "He can't very well ask you, since he's not in high school anymore."

"Yeah, I guess I will," Samantha said hesitantly. "Maybe on Saturday when he comes over to ride Sierra."

Saturday turned out to be beautiful, and the temperatures had remained warm enough that the turf course was still in good shape. Tor arrived late in the morning, after all the horses had been worked.

As Samantha met Tor at his car, she felt a wave of nervousness at the thought of asking him to the dance. She decided she'd wait until after he'd ridden Sierra. That would be a better time to bring it up. She knew she was being a coward, but as they went into the stable to collect Sierra, she put it out of her mind.

Len was already leading Sierra out, and the old black man grinned at Tor. "Going to have some fun this morning, eh? But you already know that this guy's got a bag of tricks."

Tor laughed. "Yup! I've seen him in action, but I'll give it a good shot."

Sierra was snorting and dancing across the yard at the end of the lead shank. "He's glad to be out here," Len said. "He's been out in the pasture for a few hours every day, but I have to watch him—make sure he doesn't get it in his mind to jump the fence again and go exploring."

Sierra eyed Tor as he walked to the colt's side. Tor paused to stroke Sierra's neck before he gathered the reins and mounted. "Easy, boy," he said. "We're just going out for a little jog."

"He'll probably try to buck you off once you're on the track," Samantha told Tor as she and Len walked along with him and Sierra to the inner track.

Tor grinned. "I'll be ready for anything! I'm only going to canter him. Maybe he'll behave with someone new on his back."

Len chuckled. "Oh, I wouldn't count on that."

Samantha and Len stood at the rail of the turf course as Tor warmed Sierra up. For several minutes, Samantha thought Sierra was going to surprise them and behave like an angel. But that didn't last long. A quarter of the way around the oval, he exploded in a series of bucks and tried to get the bit in his teeth. When Tor tried to put him into a canter, he refused at first. Then he lunged forward, nearly dragging the reins through Tor's fingers. Sierra made several galloping leaps up the track before Tor got him in hand again.

"He's being naughty today," Len said. "Good thing Tor knows what he's doing."

Samantha had been thinking the same thing, but she couldn't help smiling as she watched Sierra pulling his tricks on another rider. It was almost comical to see how much mischievous energy Sierra put into outwitting Tor.

Finally Tor got Sierra settled into a steady canter. It was a new experience for Samantha to watch the colt instead of riding him. She was able to see how beautifully he moved when he finally put his mind to it.

Tor took Sierra around three times at a canter, then gradually eased him back into a trot. Amazingly, Tor was smiling when he pulled the colt up beside Samantha and Len.

"Beautiful movements!" he said. "He's as headstrong as they come, but he's got incredible energy at a canter."

"He'll need to do more than canter in a steeplechase," Samantha said.

"True, but he won't need as much speed as on the flat. You could lose control if you galloped like a flat racer over the fences," Tor said. "I've got to find out more about it, of course," he added.

"But you liked the feel of him," Len said, grinning from ear to ear.

Tor laughed. "Once he settled down, I did. The rest wasn't so much fun." Tor started to dismount as Len held Sierra. As soon as Tor was on the ground, Sierra immediately snaked his head around and tried to bite him.

"So that's the thanks I get," Tor said, evading Sierra's teeth. "Watch out, or I'll take Len's advice and bite you back!"

Sierra snorted and tossed his head.

"Gotta break him of that habit," Len agreed. "It's more mischief than meanness."

"No, he's not a mean horse—just too smart for his

own good. He doesn't want to be told what to do. But his intelligence could pay off on a jump course."

"So you think he has what it takes?" Len asked.

"He might," Tor said, studying Sierra. "He just might."

They walked with the colt back to the stable yard. Len said that he'd get Sierra untacked and settled. "Why don't you go say hello to Pride," he suggested. "He's sure coming along nicely."

"We will, and I thought I'd visit Fleet Goddess, too," Samantha said, speaking of Ashleigh's beautiful racing mare who'd been retired a year before. "I can't believe she's going to be a mother this spring."

"Yup," Len said with a smile. "She's due to foal in March. I can't wait to see that foal."

"Neither can I," Samantha said.

Len led Sierra off, and as Samantha and Tor headed toward Pride's stable building, Samantha tried to get up her courage to ask Tor to the dance.

"I was wondering," she said quickly before she lost her nerve, "are you doing anything next Saturday? I mean, you don't have a show or anything?"

"No," Tor said, lifting his eyebrows questioningly.

"Well," she said in a rush, "it's just that the Christmas dance at school is next Saturday night . . . and I was wondering if you'd like to go with me."

Tor's answering smile practically turned Samantha's knees to Jell-O. "I'd love to!" he said with no hesitation. "I've been wanting to ask you to do something, but we've both been so busy . . ." He hesitated, looking awkward. "And, frankly, I was afraid you'd say no."

83

"You were afraid *I'd* say no? But so was I—I mean, I was afraid you'd say no to going to the dance." Samantha knew her cheeks had to match the color of her hair.

Tor looked at her with a twinkle in his blue eyes. "But I didn't say no."

"I could meet you at school," Samantha said, feeling hesitant again.

"Don't be silly. I'll pick you up. What time?"

"Seven thirty," Samantha said. Then they both laughed.

"It'll be fun," Tor said.

On the following Saturday, as she dressed for the dance, Samantha had a terrible case of nerves all over again. She couldn't decide what to wear. The dress she'd planned on wearing looked awful when she stood in front of the mirror. She dug through her closet for something else. The dance was dressy, and she didn't have a lot of dresses. She tried on and cast off three different outfits before ultimately settling on a dress that had been her mother's.

Samantha had always loved the simple green velvet dress—and in the last year, she'd finally grown into it. The lines were plain enough that the dress didn't look outdated, and the green matched her eyes and went well with her red hair. In her ears she wore her mother's pearl studs that her father had given her the Christmas before, and she tied up her long hair with a green velvet ribbon. She added a few light touches of makeup, but with her complexion, she didn't need much.

Then she stood in front of the mirror and carefully examined her appearance. She guessed she looked all right, although it seemed strange to see herself all dressed up.

Tor didn't know it, but today was her sixteenth birthday. Her father had already given her a present of new riding boots, which she'd been longing for, and Yvonne had driven over earlier to give her a book on jumping. If tonight turned out to be as perfect as Samantha thought it would, this would be her best birthday yet.

"You look beautiful, sweetheart!" her father told her when she finally came downstairs. He stood for a moment, staring at her with tears in his eyes. "You know, the older you get, the more you look like your mother," he said. "You're really growing up."

Samantha had to blink back tears herself. "Thanks, Dad," she said softly. "Are you sure I look okay?"

"You look wonderful! Tor's bound to be impressed." He smiled. "I think I hear a car."

Samantha froze, then unconsciously turned to look at herself in the mirror on the living room wall. She patted a few hairs in place as her father answered the door. "Hi, there," Mr. McLean said to Tor. "Come on in. Sammy's ready."

Samantha felt like a statue as Tor walked into the living room. But when he saw her, his eyes widened a little, and his lips turned up in a slow smile.

"You look great, Sammy!" he said. "Really terrific!"

"Thanks," she said shyly. Her heart started beating a little faster. She had noticed that Tor was looking incredibly handsome himself in a dark, tailored suit and tie, with his blond hair perfectly brushed. "So do you."

"Are you ready?" he asked.

She nodded and reached for her coat. "Let's go."

The dance committee had turned the school gym into a winter wonderland, and there wasn't an empty seat at any of the tables. Samantha and Tor sat with Yvonne and Jay, and Maureen and Ned Jenkins, a junior who was active on the school newspaper. The rock band, made up of Henry Clay students, was incredible. Samantha found it almost impossible to resist dancing to every song—luckily, Tor didn't want to sit any out either. They were out on the crowded floor until they were both ready to drop.

When they finally returned to the table, Samantha reached for her soda and took a long swallow. Yvonne leaned over and spoke quietly to Tor. Yvonne and Jay hadn't been dancing much, which Samantha thought was strange since they were both superb dancers. As Yvonne spoke to Tor, Samantha saw Jay frown. She wondered if he and Yvonne had had an argument, but she was having such a good time herself that she didn't want to spoil it by worrying about them.

A moment later Tor leaned over to speak in Samantha's ear. "Happy birthday!" he said.

"How did you know?" Samantha asked in surprise.

"Yvonne just told me. I wish I'd known beforehand."

Samantha glanced at Yvonne and saw that her eyes were twinkling.

"So tonight's really a special night," Tor said softly. "Have you had a happy birthday so far?"

"It's been perfect," Samantha said with a smile. "I got a new pair of riding boots, and Yvonne gave me a book on jumping." *And now that I'm here with you, my birthday is absolutely perfect,* she thought, too shy to tell him how she felt.

"Speaking of jumping," Tor said, "my father and I are going to my grandparents' in Maryland for Christmas, and I found out that their friends train steeplechasers. My grandfather's going to arrange for me to meet them and tour their place."

"Really?" Samantha said, trying to ignore the pang of regret that Tor wouldn't be around for the holidays. "You can find out everything we need to know."

"Not everything, but it'll be a big start. From what my grandfather says, his friends only have a few 'chasers in training, but they compete at some of the big meets. I can find out enough to know if you and I would be able to train Sierra."

Yvonne had been listening to their conversation. "And then you could talk to Mike," she burst in eagerly.

"That's what I was thinking," Tor agreed with a grin.

"You could work with Sierra over the winter," Yvonne added thoughtfully. "I'd love to help—"

Jay suddenly cut Yvonne short. "Don't you guys have anything to talk about except horses? Give me a break!" He pushed away from the table. "I'm going to talk to Terry about the play." He strode off across the gym.

Samantha gave Yvonne a startled look.

Yvonne shrugged and smiled wryly. "Ignore him. He's in a bad mood. Play rehearsals didn't go well this afternoon."

"We haven't been talking about horses that much," Samantha said.

"I know. Don't let him bother you. He'll get over it."

Samantha hoped Jay's mood wouldn't totally ruin Yvonne's night. Her own evening went by in a whirl of dancing and laughter. She felt completely comfortable with Tor, and she had a wonderful time.

Afterward they went with the others for burgers. It was after midnight when Tor walked Samantha to the cottage door. Before Samantha turned to go in, Tor put his hands on her shoulders and leaned down to give her a soft, gentle kiss. "Thanks," he whispered. "I had an incredible time. Happy birthday, Sammy."

Samantha's mind was reeling so much from Tor's kiss that she could hardly talk. She stared up at him with wide eyes. Finally she managed to stammer, "I had a wonderful time, too."

"I'll stop by tomorrow, okay?" Tor smiled and gently touched his finger to the end of her nose.

"Yes!" Samantha answered breathlessly.

"See you then," he said. As he turned and headed down the path, Samantha could only gaze after him in happy wonderment. She lifted her hand to her lips and sighed.

ON CHRISTMAS DAY, SAMANTHA AND HER FATHER HAD dinner at Mike's, with Ashleigh, Len, Mr. Reese, and Charlie. Samantha thought Ashleigh seemed to be glowing. She wondered why the older girl would be so happy, especially since Mike would be taking his horses to Florida in a few days for the winter races. She knew Ashleigh would miss him.

Just before they went in to dinner, Ashleigh pulled Samantha aside and said, "I didn't show you what I got for Christmas." She waved her left hand in front of Samantha's eyes.

Samantha gasped. "A ring!" she cried. "You and Mike got engaged!"

Ashleigh grinned and looked over at Mike. "We sure did," he said, beaming back at Ashleigh.

"Oh, wow! Congratulations!" Samantha hugged Ashleigh.

The men quickly chorused their congratulations,

going over to shake Mike's hand. "I was wondering when you'd get around to it," Charlie said tersely, but his blue eyes were twinkling.

"That's real good news," Len said with a wide smile. "Good news for you two and for the farm."

"I couldn't agree with you more, Len," Mike's father said.

Mike looked embarrassed by all the congratulations. Ashleigh went over to him, and he put his arm around her shoulders.

"So when's the wedding?" Mr. McLean asked.

"We haven't set a definite date yet," Ashleigh said. "We want to wait until I graduate from college this spring. I'd like to have a summer wedding, so we can set up a big tent outside."

"But nothing *too* fancy!" Mike said with a touch of panic.

Ashleigh laughed up at him. "What do you mean? We're only going to get married once!"

"It looks like I'm going to be overruled," Mike said. "Okay—a big summer wedding, but we'll have to squeeze it in between the big Belmont and Saratoga races," he teased.

They talked about the wedding plans throughout dinner. As they returned to the Reeses' living room for coffee and dessert, Ashleigh said to Samantha, "I have something to ask you. My sister, Caroline, will be my maid of honor, but I'd like you to be a bridesmaid."

Samantha flushed with pleasure. "You would? I'd love to, Ash! Thank you for asking me."

"I'm going to ask my friend Linda March, too. We

don't get to see each other as much as we used to, since she's going to college out of state, but we're still good buddies. And Jilly, Wonder's former jockey."

Samantha thought about the blond girl who first rode Wonder to fame. Jilly and her husband were living on the West Coast now.

"Aren't Jilly and Craig riding in California?" Samantha asked.

"Yes, but I hope she can take the time to come east for the wedding. I'd like our wedding to be kind of a reunion, too."

"It'll be special, I can tell you that," Samantha said. "I can't wait to tell Yvonne. She'll be thrilled. I'm so happy for you! And after you're married, you'll be living here!"

"Yup—I spend most of my time over here anyway. Actually, Mike and I have already talked about asking Clay Townsend if we could move Wonder and Townsend Princess over here, too."

"That would be incredible!" Samantha cried.

Ashleigh smiled. "It would, wouldn't it? We could be one big, happy family again."

"If Mr. Townsend agrees," Samantha said. She immediately wished she hadn't said anything. Why ruin such a happy moment by mentioning possible problems?

But Ashleigh didn't seem upset. "Speaking of weddings and the Townsends, I got an invitation in the mail yesterday."

"For Brad and Lavinia's wedding?" Samantha asked.

Ashleigh nodded. "They're getting married April

3—a huge church wedding with a reception afterward at Townsend Acres."

"Are you going?"

"I haven't decided yet—you know how I feel about Brad. I suppose Mike and I have to go to be polite. I can imagine the guest list. There'll be tons of big shots there."

"I'll bet," Samantha said. "At least I don't have to worry about being invited." Samantha knew Brad and his snobby fiancée would never stoop to invite a lowly groom and exercise rider.

As Samantha had expected, Yvonne was thrilled to hear that Ashleigh and Mike were engaged. "They're such a perfect couple," she said. "I wish I could say the same about me and Jay."

"You're only sixteen, Yvonne. If it doesn't work out with Jay, there are plenty of other nice guys—maybe even a couple who like horses as much as you do."

"Yeah," Yvonne agreed with a chuckle. "Speaking of which, when's Tor getting back?"

Samantha had felt too shy to tell Yvonne about Tor's kiss—it was too private to talk about, even to her best friend. But Yvonne had seen what a great time they'd had at the dance. "The day after tomorrow. I hope he'll have found out lots about steeplechasing."

"Me too—it'll give you something to do over the winter."

"First we have to convince Mike, and Tor's still got to get ready for the National Horse Show."

*   *   *

Tor called Samantha as soon as he got back. "I found out all kinds of stuff," he told her excitedly. "I even had a chance to watch a training session, and the Monroes said to call them anytime if I had questions. Sammy, I think we can do it! If Mike *and* Sierra cooperate, that is."

"Can you come over?" Samantha asked. "Mike leaves for Florida tomorrow, so it would be a good time to talk to him."

"Give me two minutes," Tor answerd.

When Tor arrived, he spread the papers he'd collected over the McLeans' kitchen table. "Here's the National Steeplechase schedule," he said. "There are several meets held fairly close to Lexington, and some of the major racetracks schedule steeplechases. Mr. Monroe photocopied a bunch of training articles for me, and I got a good look at his training course."

Samantha looked through the information Tor had brought. She already knew that steeplechases at the track were run counterclockwise, like flat races, over a turf course. They were longer, though—over two miles, involving two circuits around the track, with hedgelike fences set up on the course. Some of the National Steeplechase events were run over timber fences, which looked pretty threatening to Samantha, and many were run over the countryside, not on a track at all. The weights the horses were allowed to carry, including jockey, were much higher than in flat racing, so there wouldn't be any problem with Tor riding.

"Of course," Tor said, "first we've got to see how Sierra does at jumping. I figure if Mike will agree, we could van him over to the riding stable and start teaching him the basics. Then, when the weather warms up—"

Mr. McLean walked into the kitchen and came over to the table. "I've heard you two talking about steeplechasing," he said, "but I didn't think you were seriously considering it."

"We are, Dad. It may be Sierra's only chance."

Mr. McLean frowned. "You'd be biting off a pretty big chunk. I know you're an expert at jumping, Tor, but steeplechasing's a little different. You don't have the facilities—"

"We've thought of all that, Dad," Samantha said quickly. "We think we can work it all out."

Mr. McLean didn't look so certain. "And you've got no guarantees that Sierra would even take to it. He hasn't settled down at all during any of the training we've given him. What makes you think jumping will change his attitude?"

"He's proved he can jump," Samantha said. "Look how he cleared the paddock fence, and that fallen tree he and I cleared had to be at least six feet high—"

Her father stared at her. "What do you mean, at least six feet? You didn't tell me that!"

Samantha cringed. "Well, I didn't want you to worry. I mean, Sierra and I were all right, even if I did get scratched up a little."

Her father shook his head. "I don't know, Sammy." Then he added in alarm, "You're not going to be jumping six-foot fences with Sierra?"

"No," Tor assured him. "Most American steeplechase fences are more like brush jumps, about four feet high, though there are some timber-fenced courses, but we're not aiming for those right away."

Mr. McLean didn't look terribly reassured, and Samantha quickly added, "I won't be doing the jumping, Dad. I'm not good enough yet. Tor's going to ride."

"I'm glad to hear that! But I still think you both are underestimating the amount of work involved, especially when you don't have any experience at this kind of training. Look how long it takes to get a flat racer ready for the races."

"We know it's going to be hard work," Samantha said. "But we really want to try!"

Her father looked at her and smiled. "And I know what you're like, Sammy, when you get an idea in your head. All I can say is good luck."

Samantha and Tor spent another hour discussing their plans before going to talk to Mike. When they finally went next door to the Reeses', Samantha was feeling a little more confident that they could convince Mike.

Mike patiently listened to all they had to say, but he was as skeptical as Mr. McLean had been. "It's a lot of work, Sammy," he said. "I'm not sure it's worth it."

"I won't have much else to do over the winter. Pride's improving, but he won't be able to go into even light training until spring. There won't be anything going on here until February anyway, and I can always help with the exercise riding and still work with Sierra."

"I question whether Sierra will like jumping any better than he does the flat," Mike argued.

"We won't know that unless we try," Tor said.

Mike smiled. "You guys are pretty determined." He ran his fingers through his blond hair and thought about it a moment. "You say that you can start training him at your stable, Tor. No one would object?"

"Since my father and I are part owners, I don't think so."

"And you could set up fences on the turf course here in the spring?" Mike asked.

"I can easily set up fences that we can move on and off your turf course, so they won't interfere with your training," Tor said.

"How much would it cost?" asked Mike.

Samantha hadn't thought of the costs, but Tor quickly answered. "The stable could loan you the fences for the time being. If you were willing to leave Sierra at our stable while we do the early training, we'd only charge you for his feed, and you'd have to pay that anyway if he were here."

Mike still hesitated, even though Samantha thought Tor was being incredibly generous. "Please, Mike," she pleaded. "Sierra's too good a horse to give up on. Can't you at least let us try? Tor knows what he's doing."

"Oh, I'm not questioning the fact that Tor knows how to train a jumper. It's just that I know so little about 'chasing. If Sierra does show talent over fences, what kind of return are we talking about? I do know that steeplechase purses aren't as big as flat-racing

96

purses, and how much opportunity is there to race?"

"The people I met with in Maryland told me there's growing interest in steeplechasing," Tor said. "And the purses keep improving. Aside from the National Steeplechase meets, some of the big tracks have regular steeplechases. Saratoga does, and you take your string up there to race every summer anyway."

Samantha could see that Tor was wearing Mike down. She crossed her fingers behind her back for good luck.

Finally Mike shrugged. "You guys make a good argument. Okay, give it a try. I can't say I'm very optimistic about your chances—Sierra sure hasn't shown any signs of putting his mind to business. I can't see that jumping him is going to make a difference, but he'd only spend the winter eating his head off here."

Samantha felt like jumping for joy. "Thanks, Mike!" she cried. "You won't be sorry." *At least, I hope not*, she thought.

"Let me know how it goes," Mike said. "And good luck. I think you'll need it."

Once they were outside, Tor gave Samantha a spontaneous hug. "All right!" he said with a grin. "We're going places."

"Let's go tell Len and Sierra the good news!" Samantha exclaimed. "When do you think we could start?"

"The sooner the better," Tor told her, smiling down at her. "Tomorrow sounds good to me. This is going to be fun, Sammy."

"Even if you're going to be doing most of the work?"

"Oh, no," Tor told her with a twinkle in his eyes. "You know enough to ride him through the early stuff. I'll help school him over fences, but you can learn and improve your jumping right along with Sierra."

"That sounds fine to me," Samantha said, swallowing her uncertainty over her jumping abilities. "As long as you ride him in any races."

"I will."

BY THE MIDDLE OF JANUARY SAMANTHA HAD SEVERAL things to feel encouraged about. Since the Christmas dance, she and Tor had fallen into a comfortable relationship. They spent hours together during the week—now that they'd moved Sierra to the riding stable, they worked with him every day. But they were spending a lot of time together on the weekends, too, when Tor was free.

Both Samantha and Charlie had been giving Pride plenty of attention, and Pride was improving every day. Being back at Whitebrook among those who loved him helped, too.

And Sierra seemed to be enjoying his new training. The colt had been skitterish at first in his new surroundings, and he still had his bad days. But the changed routine caught his interest, and as long as he remained interested, he was quick to learn.

With Tor's guidance, Samantha had begun working Sierra on the longe line, first circling him around her at different paces. Sierra had been through all of that training and knew what was expected when he finally settled down enough to pay attention. They ended the first week's training with Samantha leading Sierra at a trot through some cavalletti. To Samantha's surprise, the colt bounced through as if he were having fun, and he caught on immediately to what was expected of him.

On the Friday of the third week, Tor had Samantha start longing Sierra over low rails. The colt was definitely showing his interest in and ability at jumping. Samantha was thrilled at Sierra's progress, but she was even more thrilled by Tor's enthusiasm. Tor was all business during the training sessions, and Samantha could see he was as excited as she was.

"In another few days, he should be ready to ride over some low jumps," Tor said.

"Do you think so?" Samantha asked excitedly.

"I always thought he was a natural jumper, and now that he's concentrating on what he's doing, I think he'll improve quickly."

Yvonne had been watching from the bleachers. She was planning to sleep over at Whitebrook that night. "Sierra's looking good!" she told them.

"I hope he does this well with someone in the saddle," Samantha said. "I'm a little nervous about that."

"I can ride him through the early jump training," Tor offered, "but you have to try, too."

"Oh, I will!" Samantha said. "But it's better if you start him. You know what you're doing."

Tor laughed. "Let's hope."

Samantha frowned for a second. "Are you sure you have the time to do this, Tor? I've been feeling a little guilty. You've got the National Horse Show coming up, and you have to start classes at college in another week."

"I've got it all figured out," Tor said. "I've got a light schedule this semester, and Top Hat and I get in a training session every day. Don't forget, the stable is quiet in the morning with the younger students in school."

"You're sure?" Samantha asked.

"Positive." He gave her a melting smile. "We're still going to the movies tomorrow night?" he asked as they led Sierra from the ring.

"Yes, sure," Samantha said, her cheeks flushing happily.

Later, as Yvonne drove them to Whitebrook, she said wistfully, "You're so lucky to have Tor. I always knew you two would be perfect together. I wish Jay and I could get along like you guys. I skipped going to his drama club rehearsal this afternoon so I could come to the stable. He was really mad."

"I hate to say it, Yvonne," Samantha said, "but Jay sounds pretty selfish to me. He wants you to care about his interests, but he doesn't care a bit that you have interests, too."

"I know," Yvonne said sadly. "He wants me to change all my plans to do what he wants. I thought he was really interesting at first because he was so intense, but now—" Yvonne shrugged. "I've pretty much decided that I'm not going to see him anymore."

"Maybe that's the right thing to do," Samantha agreed. "There are a lot of other guys who would ask you out if you weren't seeing Jay."

"You think so?"

"Come on, Yvonne," Samantha said with a laugh. "You know you're popular and fun to be with."

"Maybe I could meet someone like Tor, who likes practically all the same things I do." Yvonne paused and narrowed her eyes thoughtfully. "There *is* this one guy in my riding class. He just started, so I don't know him very well yet, but he's kind of cute, and he sure loves horses and riding."

"There you go," Samantha said with a smile. "But anyway, even if you don't find someone who loves horses as much as you do, you can still have a boyfriend who respects your interests."

Yvonne smiled too. "You're right. We'll see."

Samantha had a load of homework the following week. Her history teacher had given the class a big research assignment. But even if it meant staying up late to work on the project, Samantha squeezed in an hour each afternoon with Tor and Sierra.

On Friday, Tor got in Sierra's saddle to try him over some low jumps. He'd set up a crossbar and two single-rail fences along one side of the ring. The fences were each a couple of strides apart and were no more than a foot high. Samantha watched from the side of the arena. She had every confidence in Tor, but she had noticed that Sierra seemed to be in a naughty mood that day—he always had a glint in his eye when he was contemplating playing a few tricks. Samantha warned Tor to be prepared.

"He'll do fine," Tor assured her as he mounted the prancing colt and settled in the saddle. "He could go over those jumps in his sleep."

Samantha watched intently as Tor circled Sierra around the ring once more, then lifted in his jump seat and trotted Sierra toward the first of the fences, the crossbar. Samantha studied horse and rider. She wanted to take careful note of everything Tor did for the time when she would be in the saddle herself.

Sierra trotted forward eagerly and bounced over the crossbar with a graceful hop. They landed smoothly, and Tor cantered him two collected strides toward the next fence. Sierra smoothly cleared that, landed, cantered on, and went over the last fence with just as much ease. Tor repeated the exercise, trotting Sierra up around the head of the ring and clearing all three fences again. Sierra was tossing his head as Tor circled him.

"This is almost too easy for him," Tor said to Samantha. "Raise those poles another notch."

As Samantha did so, she noticed that Sierra had his neck arched and was pawing the ground with his front hoof.

"And I think I'll add another fence on the other side of the ring," Tor said. His brow was wrinkled in concentration. "Can you set up that dismantled fence over there?" he asked.

"Are you sure?" Samantha asked warily, frowning a little. Sierra was dancing restlessly under Tor.

"He can do it," Tor answered. "All that work on the longe line really helped."

Samantha was still uncertain as she set up the fourth jump. She knew Sierra could clear the jumps, but he was showing all the signs of getting ready to pull a fast one. Tor knew what he was doing, she reminded herself. When the jump was set up, she returned to the side of the ring to watch.

Tor circled Sierra again. They went easily over the first three jumps. Then Sierra erupted. He landed off the third jump and tried to break into a gallop. Tor acted quickly—collecting rein and sitting back in the saddle. Sierra's legs churned beneath him, but Tor had successfully checked his pace. Tor's expression was determined as he headed Sierra toward the fourth jump. Samantha could see that Sierra was furious at being checked. Just as Tor prepared to put the colt over the last jump, Sierra skidded to a sudden halt, nearly sitting on his haunches as he did. Tor went sailing over the side of Sierra's neck to land facedown at the foot of the fence.

Samantha rushed across the ring. Sierra looked incredibly pleased with himself as he eyed his fallen rider. Tor stood up, spit out a mouthful of dirt, and wiped his mouth with the back of his hand. Samantha could barely stop herself from laughing at the bewildered expression on his face. He looked down at his dusty clothing, then up at Sierra. Tor rarely fell—especially when he was jumping fences that were barely over two feet tall.

"Are you all right?" Samantha asked. She saw that Tor had managed to hold on to Sierra's reins with one clenched fist.

Tor shook his head. "He dumped me," he said, dumbfounded. "I don't believe it."

"I was afraid he was in one of those moods," Samantha said a little hesitantly.

"You devil," Tor said to Sierra. "You did that on purpose."

Sierra snorted and thrust his elegant nose in the air.

Suddenly Tor laughed. "It's been a long time since I got caught by surprise like that. Well, I guess we'll just have to try it all over again, won't we, Sierra?"

The colt gave him a baleful look.

"Don't think I'm going to let you get off with that kind of behavior," Tor told the colt. "This time you're not going to catch me unprepared!"

Sierra continued to eye Tor. Samantha went to Sierra's head and held him while Tor brushed himself off, then quickly remounted. "We'll straighten you out yet," Tor told the colt.

Sierra seemed to understand that he wasn't going to get away with the same trick again. This time, he went smoothly over all four fences. Tor praised him as he rode back to Samantha. "We'd better end it there on a good note."

"He looked really good on that round," Samantha said.

"He felt good, too. If he would only stay consistent."

Samantha sighed. "That's always been the problem with him. And we still have so much to do. We have to train him over higher fences—"

"Not too much higher," Tor put in. "With novice hedge fences, he'll only have to clear four foot or so, and we already know he can do that. He can brush right through the top of the fence. Timber fences would be different, but we're not pointing him there yet."

"But even if he starts jumping decently in the ring all the time, we still don't know how he'll do jumping on the turf course. And you're going to the National Horse Show in a week."

"There'll be time to train him when I get back." Tor smiled and put an arm around her shoulders. "Patience, Sammy. It's still only the end of January. It's not like you'll have to heavily recondition him. He's gotten enough exercise to stay fit."

"It's just that I want to be able to show him off to Mike when he gets back from Florida in March. I thought I'd bring Sierra back to Whitebrook the week you're gone and jog him on the oval to keep him fit."

"Sounds like a good idea to me," Tor said. "Don't worry, Sammy. I have a feeling this colt's going to turn into something good. Otherwise, I wouldn't be putting so much time into it."

The next morning at school, Samantha told Yvonne and Maureen about the previous day's session with Sierra. "He dumped Tor!" Yvonne exclaimed. "I don't believe it!"

Samantha laughed. "It was pretty funny, looking back at it. You should have seen the expression on

Tor's face! Anyway, Tor straightened him out. Sierra was just testing him."

"You're really getting into this steeplechasing stuff," Maureen said, pushing her glasses up on her snub nose.

"I'm learning. We've got a long way to go."

"Do you know enough to write an article about it now?" Maureen asked.

"Actually, I was thinking about that," Samantha said. "There's not much else happening this time of the year."

"When's Pride going back into training?"

"We're still not sure, but I took him out for a long walk this weekend, since the weather wasn't too bad. He's not favoring his hurt leg at all. Charlie thinks that if he keeps improving, I could start riding him at a walk next week."

"You still don't know if he's going to be able to race again, though," Maureen said with disappointment in her voice.

"No, we won't know that until he's ready to work on the track again," Samantha answered. "Sometimes a horse never comes back to form after a leg injury."

"Everyone was expecting he'd do so well as a four-year-old. There are all those big American Championship races."

"I know," Samantha said sadly. "Ashleigh and Charlie say that reporters call them all the time to see how Pride's doing, and Mr. Townsend's always over checking him. The Townsends will be really upset if Pride has to be retired from racing."

"And you won't be?" Maureen asked in surprise.

"Sure I will," Samantha said. "But I haven't given up hope."

After Maureen had gone off to her locker, Yvonne spoke quietly to Samantha. "Last night I told Jay that I didn't want to go out with him anymore."

"You did? What did he say?"

"He said that it was probably a good idea."

"And how do you feel? Are you all right?"

"At first I felt pretty bummed out," Yvonne admitted. "I kind of thought, 'Oh, gosh, what did I do?' Then I started to feel better. I mean, all Jay and I have been doing lately is arguing, and he always makes me feel like I'm the one who's wrong. I don't need it."

"I think you did the right thing," Samantha said sincerely.

"I have a riding lesson this afternoon," Yvonne added with some of her old spirit. "I'm going to try to make friends with the new guy in class. He doesn't look like he knows anyone."

Samantha chuckled. She was sure Yvonne wouldn't have any trouble breaking the ice.

10

THE NIGHT BEFORE TOR LEFT FOR THE NATIONAL HORSE SHOW
at Madison Square Garden, he came over to say
good-bye to Samantha. It was a cool evening, but
they put on their coats and went out to the stables to
visit the horses.

First they visited Pride, then Sierra, who was back
in his stall at Whitebrook so that Samantha could exercise him on the oval while Tor was gone. Then they
went to the mares' barn to see some of the newly
born early foals. "I wish I could be there to see you
and Top Hat compete," Samantha said.

Tor smiled down at her. "I wish you could, too. I'm
going to need a cheering section. I mean, my father
will be there, but that's not the same as having you
there."

The comment thrilled Samantha. She smiled back
at him a little shyly. "But I promise to watch on television. I think I'll be as nervous as you."

"I don't know about that," Tor said with a laugh. "This is the biggest show Top Hat and I have competed in, and we'll be up against all the very top riders and horses."

"You've worked so hard, and you're way up in the points standings."

"We'll do our best," Tor said, trying to hide his own nervousness. Samantha knew how much this show meant to him. As they walked and talked, they looked in over stall doors at dozing mares and a few tiny foals curled in the straw. They stopped at Fleet Goddess's stall. Ashleigh's beautiful mare was heavy with foal. Samantha felt a special bond with Goddess, since she had groomed and exercise-ridden the nearly black mare during her racing days. Goddess was the first horse Samantha had ridden after her mother's accident—and it had taken a long time to convince her father to let her ride. The mare was due to give birth the following month, and since the sire of her foal was Jazzman, Mike's prize stallion, everyone on the farm was excited. They were all keeping an extra-watchful eye on Goddess.

Goddess was dozing at the back of her stall, and Samantha didn't want to disturb her. Samantha heard a loud purr at her feet and felt a cat brush against her ankles. She looked down to see Jeeves rubbing his silky black-and-white body against her boots. She picked up the hefty male cat and rubbed her cheek against his fur. "Keeping an eye on us, are you?" she said. "I guess you left Sid and Snowshoe with Pride." Jeeves purred more deeply for a moment, but then he decided he'd had enough. He leaped from Samantha's arms up onto the partition of Goddess's stall.

"That's right," Samantha said. "She's the one you should keep an eye on."

Jeeves sat his plump hindquarters on the partition and conscientiously started grooming his left rear paw.

Samantha and Tor walked through the rest of the barn, talking easily to each other. Samantha could tell Tor's thoughts were on the competition. Before they left the dimly lit barn, he put his arm around her shoulders, then leaned over and kissed her. "I'll miss you," he said. "I'll call you from New York. When I get back, we can really concentrate on Sierra."

"I hope we'll do as well with Sierra as you're going to do with Top Hat."

Tor squeezed her shoulders. "We'll sure try!"

"Look at the height of those fences! Some of them look close to seven foot!" Yvonne cried as she and Samantha sat in front of the TV the next weekend. Yvonne had come over to Whitebrook to keep Samantha company while she watched the live coverage of the National Horse Show from Madison Square Garden. "I can't even imagine getting over those."

"Yes, you can," Samantha teased. "You're picturing yourself out there right now."

Yvonne handed Samantha the bowl of popcorn the girls had made. "What I need is my own horse, like Tor. But how could I ever afford it?"

"Start saving your money," Samantha said. "The

riders are coming out to walk the course," she added excitedly.

"There's Tor!" Yvonne cried.

Samantha had seen him. He looked handsome and professional in his tailored jacket, beige breeches, and gleaming, knee-high black boots. Her eyes were glued to his figure as he walked the course with the other riders in the top division.

This was the only opportunity the riders had to survey the course before riding out to compete. Samantha saw Tor carefully pacing out the distance between fences and trying to judge the best approach to each. The course didn't follow a simple oval. There were tight turns and switchbacks, and all the riders would be memorizing the order of the fences as well as planning their strategy in jumping them. Suddenly Samantha knew she couldn't eat any more popcorn— she was just too nervous.

"I'm glad it's not me," she said to Yvonne. "Tor must be really tense right now."

"He jumps fourth," Yvonne mused. "That's pretty early."

"I know. He won't have much of a chance to see where other riders are making mistakes. This course is much more difficult than the one I saw him jump in Louisville last year."

Then the riders were leaving the arena. Samantha crossed her fingers and silently wished Tor and Top Hat good luck. She and Yvonne sat tensely on the floor as the first rider rode into the ring, saluted the judges, and put his horse into a canter.

Samantha knew the riders would be competing against the clock as well as aiming for a clean round. Faults would count against their time, but if a rider jumped a clean round in very slow time, he could still lose.

The first rider was having trouble. His mount seemed nervous and slightly green.

"He's riding two different horses," Yvonne explained to Samantha. "This one's fairly young. His next mount's the one to watch."

The first rider left the ring with five faults. The next entrant was at the top of the national standings, and her gray mount had plenty of experience. Yet she misjudged one of the tight turns and came up short to a fence. Her mount took down a pole and was rattled as they approached the next fence. But they got over cleanly and finished the course with no further faults.

"Good ride except for that one fence," Yvonne commented. "And her time's really good."

"Tor and Top Hat will do better," Samantha said.

The next rider misjudged the water jump and fell apart through the last combination jump. Then Tor and Top Hat were entering the ring. Samantha gripped her hands together in her lap as Tor saluted the judges. "You can do it!" she whispered urgently.

Top Hat cantered alertly toward the first jump. The horse's heart and mind were obviously on the task ahead, and he looked as though he was thoroughly enjoying himself. Samantha could see the concentration on Tor's face as they made their approach to the fence. Top Hat sailed over with a seemingly effortless leap. They moved on to an oxer, over that to a two-jump combination, then into the first of the tight turns. Samantha saw Tor steadying Top Hat, choosing a slightly longer route that would bring the big horse straight on to the fence.

Samantha felt herself leaning with Tor as Top Hat gathered his hindquarters and soared. They were over and heading toward a wide jump, then a hedge, then the water jump, which would require a stretching leap from Top Hat. Samantha held her breath, but the horse cleared the water with room to spare. Already Tor was looking ahead to the next fence, beyond another tight turn. When they were over that, there were five more fences, ending with the difficult combination jump.

"How's their time look?" she whispered hoarsely.

"Good so far—if they go clean," Yvonne told her. "They lost a little time putting in the extra strides on those turns, but it'll pay off if they don't get any faults."

"Come on, guys, you can do it," Samantha murmured as Tor and Top Hat approached the last fences. They cleared one . . . then the next . . . then lift, over, land . . . lift, over, land . . . lift, over, land, and they were through the combination. "They went clean!" Samantha shrieked.

"Oh, wow!" Yvonne cried. "They're on top—the best round so far. Pray the rest of the riders get faults!"

But they didn't. Two other riders tied Tor and Top Hat. There would be a jump-off.

Samantha groaned. "Tor must be a wreck. *I'm* a wreck just watching! It's bad enough jumping that course once!"

"They'll be raising the height of the fences for the jump-off," Yvonne said. "And Tor and Top Hat ride first."

At least there are only three riders competing this time, Samantha thought. The suspense of waiting for all the riders to finish again would have killed her.

Tor and Top Hat came out. Tor looked even more determined than before—if that was possible. Top Hat was again moving with confident eagerness.

"He's an amazing horse," Yvonne said admiringly.

"And Tor's an amazing rider," Samantha added.

"I didn't say he wasn't," Yvonne protested. Then both girls were silent as they watched Tor and Top Hat start jumping the course. Tor's timing was perfect, and Top Hat's leaps were powerful and awesome to watch. They soared through the course, a picture of grace and mastery. They were still clean coming to the last combination. Then they were through it and cantering off in a circle. The audience went wild with applause. Samantha threw her fists exuberantly in the air. "All right!" she cried. She blew a kiss toward Tor. "What a beautiful trip!"

Yvonne reached over and hugged Samantha. She was grinning from ear to ear. But there were two more competitors. Yvonne settled down to watch, but Samantha was too nervous to sit down again. She paced anxiously as the next finalist went out. The rider was obviously racing the clock in order to beat

Tor, and it cost him on one of the turns, when his mount took down both top rails on the parallel jump. He jumped the rest of the course clean and in good time, but the faults put him behind Tor.

"Close," Yvonne said, "but not enough."

The last rider was being more cautious than her predecessor. She took her time on the turns. She and her mount were going clean. Samantha's throat tightened as she watched the seconds tick away.

"Unless she goes through the combination in a mad rush," Yvonne said breathlessly, "she's not going to beat Tor."

Samantha stared at the clock. The rider had a clean round, but as her final time flashed, Samantha saw that she was nearly a full second behind Tor and Top Hat.

"They won!" Samantha shouted, jumping up and down. "Yippee! Incredible! They did it!"

Yvonne was on her feet, too, and the two girls danced around, hugging. Samantha realized there were tears of happiness in her eyes. "Oh, Yvonne, I wish I were there."

"I know! Tor must be so excited! The stable's going to go wild. Tor and Top Hat winning at the National Horse Show!"

The girls turned back to the TV to watch Tor and Top Hat return proudly to the ring to collect their trophy and ribbon. The audience was on its feet, cheering them. There was no mistaking the glowing smile on Tor's face, and Top Hat was responding to the cheers, too. He arched his white neck and lifted his feet with an extra spring. Then the camera focused directly on Tor's face. He seemed to be looking right at Samantha and Yvonne from the TV screen. His smile still beaming, he took one hand from the reins and gave a thumbs-up.

"That's for you!" Yvonne cried. "He knows we're watching!"

Samantha found it hard to come down from the high of watching Tor's performance. She was so euphoric that anything seemed possible, including turning Sierra into a top-class steeplechaser.

The next morning, which was milder than usual, she and Yvonne tacked up Sierra for some exercise on the training oval.

"I'm only going to jog him," Samantha told Yvonne. "He hasn't been worked over a distance lately, and since steeplechases are all at least two and a quarter miles, we'll need to build up his stamina and keep him fit."

"He doesn't look like he's in a real cooperative mood this morning," Yvonne noted. Sierra was fighting Samantha's hold on the lead shank as they led him out into the yard, and he tried craning his head around toward Samantha for a playful bite.

But Samantha was in too good a mood to be anything but optimistic. "He'll settle down. He hasn't been outside on the track in a while. He's just excited."

"I guess," Yvonne said, eyeing the colt suspiciously. "Here, I'll hold him while you mount up."

As Samantha settled in the saddle and gathered Sierra's reins, she saw Len and Charlie approach the oval. Knowing what Sierra was capable of when he was in a frisky mood, Samantha didn't pause for a second but kept him trotting right up the track. His last weeks at the stable had done him good. He wasn't bucking and playing around as much as he'd done in the past.

"It's good to be out here, isn't it?" Samantha said to the colt. She'd missed the busy morning workouts since the cold weather had set in. Now she relished the feeling of the fresh breeze on her face and the sun on her shoulders. Sierra huffed out another breath, and Samantha let him out into a canter.

They jogged around the far turn toward the mile marker. "We'll do an easy two-mile canter today," Samantha said to Sierra. "I don't want to work you too hard, since you haven't been out here recently."

Sierra's ears flicked back as she spoke, then pricked forward again as they passed the mile marker pole. Suddenly, out of the blue, Sierra exploded and went rocketing up the track. Samantha felt herself being tossed into the air, and when she came down, there wasn't a saddle underneath her. She landed hard on her backside on the damp track. Sierra was merrily galloping away up the track, still kicking up his heels.

Samantha glared at the colt as she pulled her hands from the mud, then gradually got to her feet. The seat of her jeans and the backs of her legs were plastered with gooey muck, and the cloth stuck to her damply. She lifted one muddy fist and shook it at the departing colt. "Darn you, Sierra! Just when I was starting to feel good about you, too!"

Behind her, Samantha heard laughter and turned

to see Yvonne and Len chortling. Even Charlie had a grin on his face. "What's so funny!" she shouted angrily.

"Thought he was improving," Charlie said.

"Well, he was!"

"Boy, did you go flying," Yvonne said between giggles. "Like you were on a trampoline! You're not hurt, are you?"

"No, I'm not hurt!" Samantha stomped over to the rail, rubbing a hand over her still-smarting backside. "But I'm angry. That little monster. He waits until I least expect it! And now I've got to catch him!"

"I'll give you a hand," Charlie said. "Though he'll probably come trotting back here nice as you please, now that he's shown you who's boss."

"Well, he took off at the mile marker, where you usually ask him to gallop," Len muttered in the colt's defense.

"I'm still mad at him," Samantha said stubbornly. "And I was in such a good mood!" She looked across the track to see how far Sierra had gotten, but true to Charlie's prediction, Sierra was complacently trotting off the far turn in their direction, tossing his head. Samantha started off toward him, and he stopped dead in his tracks.

"Don't try any funny stuff, Sierra," she warned. Sierra just lifted his head and whinnied.

Len walked up beside Samantha. "I always come prepared," he told Samantha with a grin as he pulled a carrot out of his jacket pocket and waved it in the air.

Sierra's nostrils flared instantly.

119

"If you want this carrot, you've got to come get it," Len called calmly.

Sierra hesitated. His desire for play warred with the lure of the treat. Finally the colt trotted toward Len. When he reached Len's outstretched hand and started to lip up the carrot, both Len and Samantha grabbed his reins. Sierra started for a second, but he was too busy chomping the carrot to think seriously about pulling away. He followed willingly enough as they led him off the track.

"So you're set on trying to make a steeplechaser out of him," Charlie said, pushing back his hat and studying the colt. "Hope you know what you're doing."

"We're learning, and so is he," Samantha told Charlie.

Charlie grunted. "Doesn't look like he's changed his ways so far. I can't see what difference jumping him is going to make."

"He's a good jumper," she said. "He's interested in it."

"Maybe, but you've got to get him to run between the fences—and not only when he feels like it."

"Ah, Charlie," Len said, "at least give 'em credit for trying. It's a shame not to try to make something out of this colt. He's too nice a horse to give up on."

"Depends on what you mean by a nice horse," Charlie answered with a frown. "If you ask me, he's too high-minded to ever be consistent. I hate to say it, missy, but I think you're wasting your time with this steeplechasing idea of yours. It would be one thing if you had experience training or running a 'chaser—"

"You'll see, Charlie," Samantha said. "When Tor gets back, we're really going to concentrate on Sierra, and as soon as the turf course is firm enough, Mike said we can set up jumps."

Charlie shook his head. "It's your time to spend, but I'd say you're heading for a big disappointment. I can't understand Mike giving you the okay to train him. You ought to stick to something you know—put your energies into something that will pay off. This colt's never going to be worth your effort."

"Yes, he will," Samantha said, gazing at the willful colt, who at that moment was thrusting his head up, trying to pull the lead shank from Len's grasp. But she couldn't help feeling some of Charlie's doubts herself.

"At least Pride's coming along the way I hoped," Charlie added. "You won't be wasting time with him."

"You think he's ready to be ridden?" Samantha asked quickly.

"Yup. Next week. Only slow stuff at first—take him out at a walk until we see how that leg's holding up. He's not favoring it now when I lead him out for exercise, but we've got to take it easy."

11

"SO WHAT DID YOU GET? PROBABLY AN A," YVONNE SAID to Samantha as they left history class the following week. Both of them clutched their graded research projects in their hands.

"Nope," Samantha said. "Only a B plus."

"Oh—only a B plus," Yvonne said with disgust. "I worked so hard on this, and I only got a C plus! I wish I had your brains!"

"Come on, Yvonne. Brains have nothing to do with it. I just like history more than you do."

"Sure." Yvonne made a face, but her cheerful nature soon won out. "So, I'm not the best student in the world. I've got other talents, right?"

"Right! Like your personality," Samantha said with a laugh as they hurried through the crowded hallways. Yvonne was smiling and waving to most of the kids she passed. She seemed to know everyone, despite the fact that Henry Clay was a fairly big high school. "You're so friendly."

"It's easy to go up and talk to people."

"I don't think so," Samantha said.

"Speaking of meeting people . . ." Yvonne paused dramatically, then continued with a bright smile, "I had a nice conversation with that new guy at the stables yesterday. His name is Greg, and he's really into horses. He wants to buy his own horse, just like me. We could have talked for hours, but I had to get home." Yvonne's dark eyes twinkled. "He's *very* interesting."

Samantha smiled. "I'll have to come to one of your lessons so I can check him out. I guess he doesn't go to Henry Clay."

"No," Yvonne answered. "That's the only bummer. He doesn't live in Lexington, but I'll see him at the stables twice a week, and he wants to enter the spring stable show, too. Hey, you're riding Pride for the first time this afternoon, aren't you?"

"Yup," Samantha said. "Keep your fingers crossed."

"I will!"

Samantha had been worried that Pride's leg would still bother him, despite the protective wraps Charlie had put on both forelegs. But Pride moved beautifully for Samantha when she rode him up and down the grassy lane near the training barn. He walked along with smooth, flowing strides and wasn't favoring his injured leg at all.

"Oh, Pride, you're doing great," Samantha said, lovingly rubbing her hand along his neck. "I'm so relieved, boy."

Pride bobbed his head in answer. The colt, now officially a horse since he'd turned four on January 1, seemed to be enjoying their walk in the fresh air as much as Samantha was. Winter was giving up its grip as they neared the end of February, and all the horses on the farm were reacting to it.

Ashleigh and Clay Townsend had come over to see Pride's first exercise under tack. They stood at the head of the lane with Charlie, and as Samantha turned Pride and walked back toward them, she saw the smiles on their faces. Charlie looked pleased, too, as he scrutinized Pride's movements.

"He's looking good, Charlie!" Mr. Townsend said with relief as Samantha stopped Pride and prepared to dismount.

"Yup," Charlie agreed shortly. "Like I hoped."

"When do you think you can put him back into training?" Mr. Townsend asked.

"Serious training? Not for a while. If the leg stays sound, I can see putting him in light training the end of March. There are no guarantees, though. He may never run the same as he did."

"I realize that," Mr. Townsend said, "but hope for the best. A lot of people are excited about his four-year-old season. They'll be delighted to hear he's coming along. Do you think there's any possibility of him being ready for the late spring races?"

"That's counting chickens before they're hatched," Charlie said gruffly. "There's no way of knowing, and you try to rush him, it'll do more harm than good."

"I'm definitely *not* suggesting we rush him," Mr. Townsend said.

Samantha saw the relief on Ashleigh's face. She knew the older girl was thinking of all the pressure put on Pride the year before . . . and of all the disastrous results.

"I'm just thrilled to see him out here walking around," Ashleigh said.

Clay Townsend nodded happily. "We all agree on that. By the way, Ashleigh, while I'm here, I wanted to talk to you about Wonder and Townsend Princess."

He and Ashleigh turned away. Samantha strained to hear what they were saying. She prayed that Mr. Townsend wasn't going to suggest that Wonder or her yearling, Princess, should leave Ashleigh's parents' place and go back to Townsend Acres—especially when Ashleigh wanted to bring them to Whitebrook after she and Mike were married.

"Brad reminded me," Mr. Townsend said, "that we're going to have to start thinking about a training plan for Princess. She'll be broken in the fall, and obviously your parents don't have the facilities . . ."

Mr. Townsend and Ashleigh started walking away, and Samantha couldn't hear the rest of what Mr. Townsend was suggesting. She gave Charlie a panicked glance. The old trainer had overheard, too. He pursed his lips and scowled.

"Kind of figured this was coming," he said. "That little filly will have to be trained somewhere, and I can't see any reason why Townsend should agree to have her come here when he's got his own facilities."

"But—but," Samantha stuttered.

"Nothing either you or I can do about it," Charlie told her.

Samantha finished untacking Pride, but she watched Ashleigh and Mr. Townsend talking by his car. Samantha was leading Pride back to the barn when Mr. Townsend drove off. Ashleigh hurried over to her.

"Did you hear any of that?" Ashleigh asked.

"Yes," Samantha said weakly.

Ashleigh sighed unhappily. "He wants to train Princess at Townsend Acres, and there's no reason why he shouldn't, since he's half-owner."

"But you wanted to bring her here! Mr. Townsend knows you and Mike will be getting married, and you'll be living here."

"He's let us train Pride here, but he wants to train Princess at Townsend Acres, since she's a Townsend Acres horse."

"That means Brad might train her!" Samantha cried.

"There's not much I can do about it," Ashleigh said. "And I can't argue with Mr. Townsend's reasoning, Sammy. What he's suggesting is fair. We've made a compromise. I'll bring Wonder here, and Townsend Acres will take Princess." But Ashleigh sounded very depressed. "They won't be taking Princess from my parents' place for a while—it's just that I'm attached to her, and no one at Townsend Acres is . . . and I was really looking forward to training her myself. Of course, I'll have Goddess's foal, and there are a lot of young horses that Mike's bred."

Samantha knew that Mr. Townsend's suggestion *was* fair, but all she could think of was Brad and how he'd hurt Pride's career by interfering with his training. She didn't like the way Brad trained his horses. He was too heavy-handed and impatient. She wished with all her heart that Princess could have come to Whitebrook, and she knew what Ashleigh must be feeling. She was giving up the foal of her beloved Wonder to an uncertain future.

As soon as Tor returned from New York, he and Samantha brought Sierra back to the riding stable to continue his training over jumps. By the end of February Samantha was riding Sierra over steeplechase-style hedges set up around the perimeter of the stable ring.

"Keep at him!" Tor shouted as Samantha and Sierra rode through the course one afternoon. "Use your legs! Don't let him get away with that." Samantha squeezed harder, and Sierra soared over the hedge he'd already once refused. Sierra was improving, and Samantha knew *she* was improving, but she was still glad it would be Tor riding Sierra when he actually competed.

"Two more fences, Sierra. Let's go," Samantha said. She kept her head up as they approached the next hedge. Samantha knew it wasn't Sierra's fault that he'd refused the last fence. She hadn't brought him up to it correctly. This time she kept his momentum going with the pressure of her legs, and when they reached the takeoff point for the jump, she squeezed hard. Sierra lifted and soared over.

Good, Samantha thought. *Now for the last fence.* She didn't let her concentration slip, and again Sierra soared over.

"That's the way," Tor said happily as Samantha rode over to him. "When you keep after him, he gets incredible height over the fences and doesn't drag his heels through the hedge like I've seen some horses do. And your jumping is really improving, too."

"Do you think so?" Samantha asked. She couldn't have been more pleased at Tor's praise. "Sometimes I feel pretty awkward."

"Well, you still have a lot to learn—and so does Sierra—but you're getting there. The way he's been training since I got back from New York," Tor added, "I think we're ready to try him over some fences on the turf course at Mike's. Is the turf course ridable yet?"

"With all the rain we've had, it's still a little spongy. Let me check with Len and see what he thinks."

"I'd really like to get Sierra out there, so we can condition him over a true course. We might be pushing it, but there's that local steeplechase meet in Lexington in late April. There's a novice class, and since it's so close by, it might be a good place to try him out."

Samantha frowned. When she or Tor jumped Sierra over the fences in the stable arena, she really felt encouraged. Sierra put his heart into it. But she couldn't help thinking of her disappointing works

128

with Sierra on the training oval at Whitebrook and of Charlie's discouraging remarks. They had to get Sierra to run *between* fences, not just jump them. It wouldn't matter how good a jumper Sierra was if he refused to make up ground on the flat sections of a course. And the end of April wasn't that far off. But she was afraid that Mike might decide to sell Sierra if he returned from Florida and found that the colt hadn't made much progress. "We can aim for it," Samantha said. "I just wish he would show as much enthusiasm for running as he does for jumping!"

"We won't know how he'll do until we actually get him out there," Tor said.

"Right." Samantha tried to look at the bright side. "Onward and upward."

When Samantha dismounted, Tor gave her a quick hug. "We can do it!"

"And when I remember that you'll be riding, not me, I feel a lot better," Samantha said. "I still don't feel very confident with my jumping."

A week later they brought Sierra back to Whitebrook. Tor set up eight brush fences, evenly spaced around the turf course.

With spring rapidly approaching, things had picked up at Whitebrook. Samantha's father had a number of horses back in training, and Samantha and Sheldon White, Mike's other regular rider, were exercising them in morning workouts. Pride was coming along smoothly, too, although Samantha was only trotting him over the lanes. Ashleigh came over nearly every day to check on Fleet Goddess, who would soon foal, and to exercise Pride when Samantha didn't have time. Then there was all the activity in the broodmare barns, with new foals being born and the other young foals and pregnant mares to look after. Mike's father barely had a minute's free time, even with Len and Charlie to help. And there was good news from Florida. Mike called to say he was entering Wellspring in the Florida Derby in mid-March, since the colt was doing so well. He would be back at the farm by the end of March. Mike's impending return gave Samantha and Tor all the more reason to work quickly and steadily with Sierra.

Samantha had decided to work Sierra on the turf course in the afternoon since the training area was so busy in the mornings. And she also liked the privacy for Sierra's first works on the course. If he totally messed up, she didn't want everyone to know. Yvonne drove Samantha home from school on the afternoon they were working Sierra for the first time. Tor would meet them at the farm. "I should let you try driving," Yvonne said, "so you can start practicing for your license."

"You'd get in trouble," Samantha answered. "You haven't had your license long enough to teach anyone else to drive. My father and Tor both said they'd take me out when they had time, but I've been so busy with Sierra. All I can think about is having him ready for when Mike gets back."

"I can't wait to see how Sierra goes over the

130

fences," Yvonne said as they whipped along through the greening countryside.

"Don't get your hopes up too high," Samantha warned. "You remember what he did to me the last time you watched me work him on the oval."

"Yeah, but this will be different. He'll have the jumping to keep him interested. Tor's going to ride, isn't he?"

"We both thought it would be better if he did—at least until I build up my own confidence. Jumping on the turf course will be a new thing for Sierra. He needs an experienced rider."

Tor was already at Whitebrook talking to Len when the girls arrived. Len had Sierra tacked and ready to go. Sierra was prancing on the gravel, invigorated by being outside on a beautiful afternoon.

"I hope he's not going to be a handful," Samantha said as she studied the colt.

Tor smiled as they walked up. "I got here early so I could double check the fences. Sierra's all set."

"Let's go, then," Samantha said. She couldn't help feeling a little nervous about what might be ahead. Tor didn't seem worried.

They walked Sierra out to the inner turf course. Tor had set up the jumps so that there was plenty of room along the outer edge of the oval to warm up Sierra on the grass surface.

Samantha held Sierra as Tor mounted. "Behave yourself," she told the horse. "What you're doing today is important."

The colt just eyed her.

"He'll do fine," Tor said, gathering the reins and winking at Samantha. "Come on, fella, let's show her."

Samantha was relieved to see that Sierra did seem to be behaving himself as Tor warmed him up. Of course, the biggest test was still ahead. Samantha, Yvonne, and Len stood back against the outer rail of the turf course as Tor finished the warm-up and paused briefly beside them.

"I know he's going to eventually have to do the course at a gallop, but I think I'll try it at a canter today."

Samantha watched nervously as Tor put Sierra into a canter, then headed him up around the oval toward the first fence. Since the turf course was just short of a mile, there was approximately a furlong between each of the eight fences.

Samantha felt her hopes soar as Sierra went over the first fence without hesitation and set out smoothly for the next. Tor was sitting coolly in the saddle in more of a crouch than he used in the show ring. They went on to the second, third, and fourth fences. They were in the middle of the backstretch, and suddenly Sierra broke stride and tried to spurt toward the next fence. He roared up on the hedge, but somehow Tor got him over without losing his seat. Sierra's strides were uneven after that, and Samantha could see that he was fighting for rein. She wondered if the colt was confused at being out on the course where he was normally asked to gallop, and was now being asked to jump. Tor and Sierra came off the far turn with one fence left. Sierra was unsettled now. He took off too soon and dragged his hind feet through the top of the hedge. The brush easily gave way, but Sierra was definitely upset as Tor pulled him up. "I think I tried too much too soon," Tor said with a worried frown. "He did the first half beautifully, but then he fell apart."

"He was confused," Samantha said.

"I think he was," Tor answered. "What I probably should do is take out some of the fences, then gradually work him up to more jumps and a longer distance."

"I was thinking the same thing," Samantha said. She reached over and cautiously patted the colt's nose, but he was too distracted to make any attempt at playful biting. "You tried hard today, fella. You'll do better."

"I hope so," said a voice from behind her.

Everyone started and turned to see Mike standing at the gap to the turf course.

"Mike!" Samantha cried. "We didn't think you'd be back until after the Florida Derby. Welcome home!"

"Thanks," Mike said with a smile. "I decided to come up for a few days. The horses are all set for the moment, and the new groom I hired is working out really well, so I felt safe leaving the horses in his hands. I'll be back in plenty of time for the Florida Derby." Mike paused. "But I thought you might have made more progress with Sierra. I admit I don't know much about steeplechasing, except for having watched some 'chases at Saratoga, but he looked pretty uncertain and uneven to me. Do you really think he's going to do better over fences than he did on the flat?"

133

Samantha felt her stomach sink. "It's the first chance we've had to work him on the course," she explained. "We've been training him at the stables. He's really showing talent as a jumper. He just wasn't real sure what was expected of him today."

Mike lifted his fair brows skeptically. Samantha knew he was remembering Sierra's past training record. He didn't really think they could turn the colt around.

"Give us a little more time, Mike," she pleaded. "He really is showing promise."

After a moment, Mike shrugged. "Okay. But I hope he'll have made some improvement by the time I get back from Florida next time. Otherwise, I'm going to have to give up on him. Things will be getting really hectic around here, and we'll have other young horses who'll need the time and attention you're putting into Sierra. You can't win them all. Well, I've got to go meet Ashleigh," Mike said with a final smile. "See you guys later."

When Mike was gone, they all exchanged worried glances. "I guess we'll have to work at it doubly hard now," Samantha said.

"I guess so," Tor agreed, scowling.

12

AND THEY DID WORK HARD. TOR COULDN'T GET OVER every afternoon because he had college classes to attend and riding classes to teach. And there were several days of heavy rain, during which they couldn't get out on the grass course at all. But the March days were growing longer, and soon it was light enough in the late afternoon for Tor to squeeze in some quick sessions with Sierra after his classes. When he couldn't get to Whitebrook, Samantha took Sierra out over a partial course, but she wasn't confident enough of her jumping abilities to put Sierra over more than a couple of fences.

With Tor in the saddle, Sierra was improving. Now that Sierra understood that he was expected to jump on the course he'd only galloped over in the past, he'd settled in. But they still couldn't get him to be consistent. His jumping was fine. His speed between the fences wasn't.

"He needs to jump against another horse," Tor said.

"He needs to know that this isn't just play—it's a race."

"We tried running him with pace horses when he was in flat training," Samantha reminded him. "It didn't help. He just fooled around and tried to bite the other horse."

"But he's more interested in what he's doing now," Tor said.

"But we don't have another jump horse."

Suddenly Tor's eyes lit up. "Maybe I can work something out. My father's got a hunter coming along. Our problem has been *stopping* him from galloping between fences. He's still kind of green, but maybe—"

"You want to bring him over here?" Samantha asked.

Tor grinned. "Yeah. I don't think he's got racing potential, and he sure hasn't got Sierra's bloodlines, but maybe if Sierra saw a horse galloping next to him between the fences, it would wake him up."

Samantha wasn't sure it would work, but anything was worth a try, with Mike due to return from Florida the following week.

The next day was Sunday, so Tor had no classes to teach. He used his stable van to bring the hunter over. Cisco was a five-year-old, pure gray Thoroughbred gelding. He obviously had a more mannerly disposition than Sierra. He came calmly out of the van, then stood quietly and gazed around with interest at his new surroundings while Tor tacked him up.

But he had gumption, too. When Len led Sierra out and introduced the two horses, Sierra immediately tried to take a nip at Cisco's neck. Cisco bit back, and Samantha, Tor, Yvonne, and Len burst out laughing at Sierra's confounded reaction. He stepped back, snorting and staring in total bewilderment.

"That'll teach you," Samantha said, still laughing. "Maybe now you'll learn that you can't go around biting. There are some horses who bite back."

Sierra snorted again and looked at Cisco warily.

Samantha turned to Tor. "Do you want to try the whole course after we warm them up?" she asked a little hesitantly. She was nervous. She'd never jock-eyed Sierra over a full course.

"Let's try it—see how we do after one circuit. If they're doing okay, we might as well keep them going."

Samantha nodded. Len held Sierra as Samantha mounted and settled herself in the saddle. She just prayed Sierra would behave himself.

When Tor was mounted, they rode out onto the turf course and warmed the horses up at a trot and a canter around the perimeter of the oval. Sierra behaved well enough. Samantha saw him eyeing Cisco, but at least Sierra seemed interested.

As they finished lapping the track, Tor looked over at Samantha. "Ready?" he asked.

"As ready as I can be," she said, swallowing nervously.

"Let's do it, then."

They stopped the horses at the marker pole and readied themselves. "Go!" Tor called.

Samantha leaned over Sierra's withers, gave him rein, and tightened her legs on his girth. He bounded forward. Cisco jumped out with him, and together the two horses pounded up the grass course. Samantha kept a firm grip on the reins and looked ahead to the first fence. Through repeated practice, she had learned how to gauge the right takeoff point, although that was no guarantee she and Sierra would go over cleanly. But they hit the first fence perfectly. Samantha squeezed with her legs, gave rein, and they flew over, landing and galloping on to the next fence. Tor and Cisco were right beside them as they jumped the next four fences and came down the backstretch with three more fences in the first circuit.

Using Cisco as a pace horse seemed to be working. Sierra's strides were steady and even. He wasn't backing off. Samantha doubted they could have won any races at their present speed, but she was still relieved. "Keep it going like this, Sierra," Samantha murmured, "and I'll give you a kiss when we're done."

Together she and Tor landed off the eighth fence. Samantha glanced over at Tor and saw him put his thumb up, his signal to try another round. Samantha mentally geared herself for the second circuit. Sierra wasn't showing any signs of wanting to stop. He was energetically striding toward the first fence for their second round.

They cleared the fence cleanly, then Tor and Cisco started drawing away, gaining a length's lead. *What's he doing?* Samantha thought frantically. Then she realized Tor was picking up the pace to see if Sierra would follow suit.

Sierra reacted immediately. When he saw Cisco drawing away from him, he instantly lengthened his stride and surged after the other horse. But with the faster pace, Samantha knew they would meet the fence differently. For an instant she panicked, afraid she wouldn't be able to get Sierra over. She gritted her teeth with determination. She would do it! And Sierra was actually helping, adjusting his own stride as they flew up toward the fence. They sailed over, and Samantha relaxed a little—but not much. There were six more fences to clear.

Tor kept the pace brisk as he and Cisco galloped on. But by the fifth fence, Sierra and Samantha had caught up to them. Samantha thought she saw Tor smile when he saw them come pounding up beside him, but she had all her attention focused on the next fence. Sierra was pulling at the reins, ready for more. He was striving to get ahead, not just to stay even with Cisco. Samantha couldn't believe it.

Well, why not? she thought. She called softly to Sierra. "Okay, have it your way. Let's beat them, Sierra!" The colt's ears were back, and when Samantha lightly kneaded her hands along his neck, he turned up his speed another notch. Samantha knew that what she was doing was risky. Her skill over the jumps was only moderate, but now that Sierra was actually putting his heart into it, she didn't want to pass up the opportunity of testing him.

Her eyes were focused on the next fence as they roared up to it. She checked Sierra slightly to shorten his stride, but Sierra was one step ahead of her, adjusting on his own, then lifting and soaring. Samantha forgot all of her earlier nervousness and got into the spirit of the race. Tor hadn't caught them yet. She didn't dare look back to see how much of a lead she and Sierra had. She wasn't confident enough to take her eyes off the course for even an instant.

"Two more to go, Sierra!" she called excitedly. "You're doing great. Keep on going, boy!" The colt did. They raced around the far turn, flew over the second-to-last jump, and came off the turn toward the last jump. Samantha had been afraid that Sierra would lose interest once he had a firm lead, but he was still running like the wind! *Over this fence, and a gallop down the stretch*, she thought.

But with her growing confidence, she got lax. She'd brought Sierra up too close to the last fence. He courageously collected himself and got them over, but Samantha bounced badly in the saddle as they landed and lost a stirrup. She was determined not to give up now, though. She gripped Sierra's sides with her legs and urged him on down the stretch. *If I can just hang on until the marker pole*, Samantha thought, *that's all I care about.*

As they tore down the stretch, she saw Yvonne and Len standing along the rail with expressions of amazed disbelief on their faces. She watched the marker pole, too, and as they flew past it, she leaned back in the saddle and drew on the reins. She hadn't thought until that moment about how she was going to get Sierra to stop, especially since she couldn't stand in the irons. What if he didn't stop and tried jumping the course again? And she only had one stirrup!

But for a change, Sierra instantly obeyed the signals

Samantha gave and dropped back into an energetic canter, then a trot. Samantha slid her foot back into the stirrup as she turned Sierra to head back to the gap.

Tor rode toward her. His face was wreathed in smiles. "I couldn't believe it," he said with a laugh. "At first I thought he'd bolted with you."

Samantha grinned back at him, still exhilarated from the race. "Nope. He just wanted to run and beat Cisco. You did a fantastic job, boy, didn't you? For a change!" she added as she firmly patted Sierra's neck. The colt snorted and tossed his head. But now that the ride was over, Samantha was beginning to realize what she'd done. Had she actually gone tearing over those fences at breakneck speed?

Tor chuckled when he saw her expression. "It's sinking in, huh? Didn't think you could do it, did you?"

"I'm having trouble believing I *did*! I almost lost it at that last fence, though."

"I saw. I thought for sure you would be taking a header, but that's where Sierra's intelligence shows. He knows how to correct."

Yvonne and Len hurried over. "Amazing!" Yvonne exclaimed. "He was running like he was enjoying it!"

"He was enjoying it," Samantha said happily.

"I always knew this monster would come around," Len added as he rubbed a weathered hand over Sierra's neck. "Glad they didn't give up on you."

"Of course, one good work over the jumps doesn't mean he's going to be a success," Tor said. "We still have a long way to go."

"But today sure gives me a lot more encouragement to keep trying," Samantha added. "When Mike gets home in a few days, we'll have something to show him."

Tor stayed for the rest of the afternoon, and together they went over their plans. Samantha was on a high. Finally, they were making progress! As soon as they got Mike's permission—and Samantha was hopeful now that they would—they'd enter Sierra in the local novice steeplechase at the end of April.

"This local steeplechase is strictly for amateurs," Tor told Samantha. "The jockeys aren't required to be licensed, and I don't think there's any prize money, but it'll be good experience for him and for me."

"And if he does well . . ."

Tor smiled brightly. "Then we can start looking at the sanctioned novice events and see if Mike will bring him up to Saratoga this summer. Since he's only three, he won't be eligible for a lot of steeplechases this year."

Samantha nodded. She knew that most steeplechases were restricted to four-year-olds and up, and most of the horses competing were five or older. Steeplechasers competed much longer than flat racers. "But the idea of Sierra running in any race is so exciting!" she exclaimed. "We did it! We turned him into a steeplechaser!"

Tor reached over and squeezed her hand. His blue eyes were sparkling. "He needs a lot more practice—and so do I if I'm not going to make a fool of myself. Pray it doesn't rain much for the next few weeks so I can get out on the course with him!"

Samantha was getting ready for bed that night

when there was a loud knock on the front door. Her father was still downstairs, and he answered it. Samantha stepped out into the hall and looked down the stairs, wondering who would be coming to the cottage so late. A moment later her father called up to her. "Sammy! Get dressed. That was Ashleigh. Fleet Goddess is having her foal. She thought you might want to be there."

"I sure do want to be there!" Samantha dashed back into her bedroom, pulled off her nightgown, and quickly put on jeans, a sweatshirt, and boots. A minute later she was rushing back downstairs. "Are you coming, too, Dad?" she called.

"No, I'll stay here. There'll be enough people around. I'd only add to the confusion."

"See you later, then," she said breathlessly as she rushed out the door toward the mares' barn. Len and Mr. Reese were outside Goddess's stall with Ashleigh. So were two of the cats, Snowshoe and Jeeves. Ashleigh turned when she heard Samantha approach.

"How's she doing?" Samantha asked.

"Fine so far," Ashleigh said with a nervous catch in her voice. "Len thinks it's going to be a fast birth. I hope it's an easy one, too, for Goddess."

Samantha and Ashleigh looked over the stall door. The beautiful nearly black mare was on her side in the straw. She grunted as a contraction pushed her foal closer to birth.

"Won't be long now," Len said. "Why don't you go on in with her, Ashleigh. She'll be less anxious with you there."

143

Ashleigh quickly let herself inside the stall, walked quietly to Goddess's head, and knelt beside her. "It's going to be all right, girl," Ashleigh said soothingly. The mare nickered a weak greeting, then grunted again as another contraction gripped her. Len entered the stall now, too, and stood behind Goddess, ready to help if the foal needed it.

"The forelegs are starting to show," he said with quiet excitement. "Another couple of contractions should do it."

Ashleigh rubbed her hand over Goddess's sweat-drenched neck. Samantha could see the worry on Ashleigh's face, and her own stomach felt as though it was tied in a knot. Goddess had been special to her ever since Ashleigh had first brought the mare home to Townsend Acres. Samantha had seen other foals born at Whitebrook and knew the many things that could go wrong, but Goddess was young and strong, she told herself. Everything would be all right.

Goddess grunted again and lifted her head off the straw as her body fought to release her foal.

"All right there, girl," Len said. "Not much longer now." He knelt in the straw beside Goddess. Samantha saw that the foal's head had emerged, still covered in the white birth sack. "One more good push, little lady," Len said encouragingly, "and your work will be over."

Goddess heaved again, and Samantha gazed in wonder as Goddess's foal slipped fully into the world. Already its tiny nose was pushing through the birth sack. Goddess gave a delighted whicker as she craned her head around and saw her foal for the first time. The newborn was struggling to free itself from the sack.

"This is a strong little one," Len said with satisfaction.

Goddess thrust her head forward to touch her nose to the foal's. Then she began to lick the tiny wet body.

"A filly!" Len said.

Ashleigh let out a happy sigh. "All right!"

"She's beautiful," Samantha murmured. She couldn't take her eyes off the tiny, wet bundle. "She looks like she's going to be a true black, like Jazzman."

"Yup," Len said, "but she's got a white triangle on her forehead, like her dam."

Ashleigh and Len stood to give Goddess and her newborn more room. "I don't think they need our help," Len said. "The two of them are doing just fine."

"It sure looks that way," Mr. Reese agreed.

They all watched as Goddess continued to lick her foal dry. After a few minutes, the mare carefully rose and continued her ministrations. The little filly's oversize ears flicked back and forth as she gazed about at her new world. Finally her fuzzy coat was dry. Goddess nickered her encouragement as the tiny filly began gathering her long, gangly legs beneath her. She pushed up with her forelegs, then tried to lift her hindquarters. Her little body strained and swayed. She was almost up when she suddenly wobbled badly and fell in a heap in the straw. But soon she was pulling her overlong legs beneath her to try again.

"That's a girl," Samantha said. She noticed that the cats had jumped up on the stall partition and were watching. They seemed as enthralled as the humans.

Goddess made soft, coaxing noises, and the foal got her forelegs under her again and heaved her tiny body up. A moment later, she was standing unsteadily, with feet spread wide on the straw. But she was up. Her big ears flicked back and forth as if she was amazed at her feat. Goddess touched her nose to the foal's and continued coaxing. The filly took a small step, tottered drunkenly, and nearly fell. Somehow she managed to stay upright, steadied herself, and tried again. This time her uncertain step brought her to her mother's side.

"She's going to be a bright one," Len said with all the pride of a doting uncle. "Real precocious she is."

Samantha saw that Ashleigh's eyes were shining, and there was a flush of happiness on her cheeks. Ashleigh looked over at Samantha and smiled. "Precocious! How's that for a name? It does fit her. She's ahead of most newborn foals I've seen."

Samantha grinned back. "I like it."

"Precocious you are," Ashleigh said, turning to the foal, who was already trying to nurse. "You'll help make up for Princess being sent to the Townsends. And the Townsends don't have any claim on you!"

Precocious flicked her tiny brush of a tail, then settled down to the serious business of nursing.

13

MIKE RETURNED FROM FLORIDA ON TUESDAY. SAMANTHA stood nervously beside him the next afternoon as they watched Tor take Sierra through two flawless circuits over the jumps. She had been afraid that without a pace horse to prod him, Sierra would lose interest again. But he was running between the fences with the spark and determination of a horse whose mind was on business! Mike looked dumbstruck when Tor finally trotted Sierra off the course.

"I never dreamed you could do it!" Mike exclaimed, gaping at Sierra, who looked none the worse for having galloped nearly two miles and jumped sixteen fences. "He doesn't look like the same horse I saw two weeks ago. He's running like he wants to."

"He *does* want to," Samantha said. She was incredibly relieved that Sierra hadn't let them down, and proud of what they'd accomplished.

"I'm impressed," Mike said. "I just hope the performance he put in today wasn't a fluke."

"It wasn't," Samantha said, although she realized that Sierra had been inconsistent in the past.

"What's next?" Mike asked.

"There's a novice steeplechase in Lexington at the end of April," Samantha explained. "It's not a sanctioned meet, but we thought it would a good place to start Sierra and give him some experience—if you agree to running him," she added, anxiously watching Mike's face.

"Right here in town, huh?" Mike rubbed his chin thoughtfully. "We wouldn't have to worry about shipping and stabling expenses. It sounds like a good opportunity for him to prove himself. All right, why not? But I'll tell you honestly that if I'm going to put any more time and money into him, he's got to do well. This will be his last chance. In fact, I was talking to a breeder in Florida who might be interested in buying him for stud if I decide to sell."

Mike's last words sent Samantha's heart plummeting to her feet. "The race is Sierra's last chance?" she exclaimed. She couldn't believe she'd heard him correctly.

"I know how you feel about him, Sammy," Mike said, "but I have to look at it from a business standpoint. As much as I appreciate what you've done with him, I can't afford to enter him in races when it doesn't look like he's going to win."

"I know," Samantha cried. "But he's come so far—"

"I haven't written him off yet. He still has an opportunity to prove himself in this local 'chase." Mike paused and studied Sierra. "If he does do well in this, where do we go from there?"

Tor answered for Samantha. "There are some National Steeplechase meets in nearby states in late spring, and there's Saratoga in late summer."

"I'll be bringing horses up to Saratoga anyway," Mike said thoughtfully, "so that sounds like a possibility. Of course, it all depends on how he does in this novice race."

"Racing over fences has made all the difference with him," Samantha said quickly. "You'll see." She wished she was as sure as she sounded. It was urgently important for Sierra to do well.

"I hope so," Mike replied. "I won't make any decisions until after the race. So what do you think of Fleet Goddess's foal?" he asked in a lighter tone.

"Oh, she's a beauty!"

Mike flashed a brilliant smile. "She is, isn't she? She looks like she's inherited the best qualities of Goddess and Jazzman. She's a perfect coming-home present for me, especially after Wellspring only ran fourth in the Florida Derby."

"But he put in a good race," Samantha said. "He was closing fast and lost by only two lengths."

"I know," Mike agreed. "He's a distance horse, but I don't think he'll be ready for the Kentucky Derby. Well, there's always next year. We have some nice two-year-olds coming along." Mike gave Sierra a final pat. "Thanks again for all your work with him. Let's hope he lives up to it."

When he was gone, Samantha and Tor exchanged a worried look.

"Mike sounded pretty definite that this is Sierra's last chance," Tor said.

Samantha was still reeling. "Yeah—I'm afraid he means it."

Tor ran a hand through his blond hair. "It really puts the pressure on us."

Samantha turned to Sierra. "You just better keep going like you are," she warned. "You've *got* to do well in the steeplechase. You don't know how important it will be!"

The colt thrust his nose in the air.

"Three and a half more weeks and we'll find out," Tor said.

Over the next few days, Samantha or Tor worked diligently with Sierra every afternoon, sharpening his technique and building his stamina. They couldn't push him too hard, since they didn't want to burn him out. Their aim was to have him in top form by the end of April. But Samantha sometimes felt there was a time bomb ticking away, set to go off if Sierra flopped in the upcoming steeplechase.

On Monday morning Charlie decided that Pride was ready to go on the oval for his first light work. "We'll just trot him today," the old trainer told Samantha. "He's going to need time to get back into condition, but he's come back from that injury better than I thought he might."

It was such a joy to be in Pride's saddle out on the oval again that Samantha could almost forget her worries about Sierra. Pride loved being back on the

150

track, too. He pranced eagerly in the warm sunshine, with ears pricked and a spring in his stride. Samantha could feel that he was anxious to do more than trot, but he willingly obeyed her when she held him to the slower pace.

"He felt wonderful!" she said to Charlie as she rode off the track after two laps. Ashleigh was standing with the old trainer. From the glow on Ashleigh's face, Samantha knew how pleased the older girl was.

"He *looks* wonderful!" Ashleigh cried. "He's moving like he never had an injury!"

"Yup," Charlie agreed. "But we'll have to see if that's the case when he puts more stress on the leg. I figure a week of trotting, and maybe we'll be ready to try him at a jog."

"I don't want to rush him," Ashleigh said.

"You don't have to tell *me* that, missy," Charlie answered gruffly. "I just hope the Townsends cooperate."

"Mr. Townsend will," Ashleigh said. "He's already said he doesn't want to pressure Pride."

"It remains to be seen if he'll stick to that once this guy starts serious training." Charlie knelt beside Pride, removed the bandage, and felt Pride's leg. "It feels good. No heat at all," he said. Then he turned back to Ashleigh. "So how was the Townsend kid's wedding yesterday? As big a shindig as you expected?"

"Bigger," Ashleigh answered. "You should have gone, Charlie, and seen for yourself," she added in a teasing tone. "You were invited."

"Bah—not my kind of thing!"

"Well, all the big shots in racing were there. There

151

were two bands at the reception, and enough food to feed all the poor in Lexington for a year. And they had a huge fountain in the middle of it all, spouting champagne."

"How did Lavinia look?" Samantha asked.

"Gorgeous. I'd hate to think what she paid for her gown—it was a designer original. The train must have been twelve feet long. But listen to this. Guess what she gave Brad for a wedding present?"

"A new Ferrari?" Samantha asked with a laugh.

"Something more expensive than that."

"What, then—a new house, another farm?" When Ashleigh shook her head, Samantha asked, "Not a racehorse?"

"Yup. And not your ordinary racehorse. She bought Brad last year's top English three-year-old, Lord Ainsley."

"But she must have paid a fortune!" Samantha exclaimed.

"She did," Ashleigh said. "Over a million dollars, and Brad plans to race him here this year. The horse is already at Townsend Acres."

"Did you see him?" Samantha asked.

Ashleigh nodded. "Mike and I went down to the stable after the reception. Brad couldn't wait to show Lord Ainsley off to everyone. He's a beautiful horse—a dark bay with perfect conformation. He looks like a champion."

"But that means Brad will probably be racing him against Pride, if Pride comes back to form," Samantha said.

"Right," Ashleigh answered.

"Just what you need—to be competing against Brad!"

"We've competed against each other before, when Wonder and Townsend Prince were racing, and believe me, it wasn't fun."

Charlie shook his head at the two of them. "You're jumping out of the gate too fast," he said gruffly. "First of all, we don't know if Pride's even going to make it back to the races. Second, the English horse may not take to our tracks over here. English tracks are altogether different. Besides—having another top horse to train might keep the Townsend kid from sticking his nose in *our* business, which would be real *good* news!"

"Maybe," Ashleigh said. "But it could also make things a lot worse. Brad won't want Pride to succeed if he's got his own horse running for Townsend Acres."

"Pride's got a long way to go before we can even think about entering him in a race, or worry about who he's going to race against," Charlie told her.

"Yeah, you're right, Charlie," Ashleigh said, "but anything connected with Brad makes me nervous. I can't help it. He always seems to mess things up for me."

"I haven't forgotten the difficulties you've had with the Townsends," Charlie admitted, "but there's no point in getting yourself in a fret over it before it happens."

Samantha dreaded the thought of more problems

153

with the Townsends, but for the moment she had Sierra's steeplechase to concentrate on. To Samantha's immense relief, the colt continued training well. Sometimes Samantha felt like pinching herself to see if she was dreaming. Was this actually the same horse she'd had so little success with in the fall? But Sierra and Tor were getting better with each practice session. Their time over the fences kept improving, and amazingly, they had no falls or other mishaps. Samantha was almost afraid that things were going too perfectly.

Pride was progressing, too. After a week of trotting him on the oval, Charlie told her to try him at a jog. Pride worked eagerly at the faster pace. He didn't favor his right foreleg at all. After two miles at a jog, the leg showed no signs of stress, and Samantha could feel that Pride was ready for more.

Clay Townsend had come over to watch and was just as thrilled that Pride seemed sound. "If he keeps coming along like this," he said to Charlie, "he just might be ready to run in midsummer. We could enter him in the last of the American Championship races and head him toward the Breeders' Cup again."

The next afternoon, as Samantha was changing out of her school clothes in preparation for Sierra's daily workout, the phone rang. She picked it up from her bedroom nightstand.

She heard Tor's voice. "Sammy, I've got some bad news."

Samantha froze. "What's wrong?" she cried.

"I've broken my arm."

"Oh, no! What happened? Did you take a spill?"

"Believe it or not," Tor said miserably, "I was helping my father store a shipment of hay. I was stacking the bales, stepped back, and fell. I heard the bone in my arm snap when I landed."

"Oh, Tor! Does it hurt?"

"Like heck! I just got back from the hospital. But Sammy, the worst part is that I can't ride—not for weeks!"

Samantha sat down with a jerk on her bed. She tried to absorb what Tor was saying. "Sierra's steeplechase is in less than two weeks," she said in a dazed tone.

"I won't be able to ride, Sammy. You're going to have to."

"But I can't! I'm not good enough!"

"You can be," Tor told her.

"No—I don't have enough confidence. I'd ruin Sierra's chances! Besides, I don't know if my father would let me. We'll have to take him out of the 'chase, Tor."

"Remember what Mike said. This may be Sierra's only chance," Tor argued.

"How could I forget?" Samantha groaned.

"And it's the best opportunity he'll have for a while," Tor continued. "There aren't that many novice events. If we miss this race, we'll have to ship out of state to race, and I doubt Mike would want to do that when Sierra's still unproven. You *can* do it, Sammy! And I'm sure we can convince your father.

You're much better over fences than you think you are. Look how well you rode when I brought Cisco over."

"I just acted on impulse then. I'd be an absolute wreck if I had to ride in a real jump race."

"I'll help you," Tor said. "I've already talked to my father. He said he'd take over most of my classes for the next two weeks so I can come to Whitebrook as soon as you get home from school. I can still drive an automatic. You're a good rider, Sammy, and you can handle Sierra."

"It would be different if it were a flat race," Samantha said. "I'd feel confident then."

"So it'll be a little harder, but don't forget that the other riders will all be amateurs, too."

"And they probably all have more experience jumping."

"Then think of Sierra. After all the work you've done, you don't want him to miss his chance."

Samantha took a deep breath. No, she couldn't let Sierra down now—not when it meant Mike might totally give up on him and sell him. "Okay," she said uncertainly. "I'll try."

"That's the spirit!" Tor said. "I'm not feeling too swift this afternoon, but I'll pick you up at school tomorrow, and we'll start right in. Okay?"

Samantha swallowed hard. "Okay."

Samantha hung up and finished changing out of her school clothes, then went out to the stable to Sierra's stall. He was chomping on his hay, but stuck his head curiously over the half-door as she approached. Seeing her, the colt snorted eagerly.

"Well, boy," Samantha said miserably, "we've got *more* problems. You're finally doing great, and Tor gets hurt!" She was so stunned, she could barely think straight. It still hadn't fully sunk in that she would have to ride in the steeplechase.

As she stood staring into space, Len came up behind her. "Looks like you've got something on your mind," he said.

"I do, Len." She told him about Tor's accident. "I can't believe I'll have to ride the colt in the 'chase," she added.

"You don't think you can do it," Len said.

"I'm scared to death," Samantha admitted.

"Look, I've seen you take Sierra around the course, and you *are* good enough. You just need to build up your confidence."

"That's the hard part. I don't want to ruin Sierra's chances."

"You've got nearly two weeks till that 'chase, and there's no time like the present to make a start in building up your confidence. Sierra's ready to go out there."

Samantha looked over at the colt, then straightened her shoulders. *I can do it*, she told herself. *I have to*. She took a deep breath.

"Okay, Len. Let's tack him up."

14

"OH, NO!" YVONNE SAID THE NEXT MORNING WHEN SAMAN-tha told her about Tor. "Does that mean you're not going to run Sierra in the race?"

"It means *I'm* going to ride him."

"All right!" Yvonne said excitedly. "I mean, I'm sorry about Tor, but I think it's great that you get to ride Sierra!"

"I'm scared out of my mind!"

"I'm always scared before a show, and I always do fine."

"This is a little different," Samantha argued.

"Why?"

"Because there will be a bunch of other horses and riders out there with me. I don't just have to get Sierra over the jumps, I have to avoid the other riders, find the right spots to jump and try to stay on his back—all while we're moving along at a gallop. And you know Mike said this is Sierra's last chance. What if I blow it for him?"

"I have an idea," Yvonne said. "We'll get Tor to bring Cisco over to Whitebrook. I'll ride Cisco and give you as much trouble as I can so you and Sierra can get used to it."

"Right," Samantha said with a laugh. "I can just see you cutting me off on the turns."

"Well, I wouldn't do anything too drastic, but it would give Sierra more of a feel for what an actual race would be like."

"There'll be more than two horses on the course when he races." Samantha paused thoughtfully. "But I suppose it couldn't hurt. Let me ask Tor."

Tor thought it was a great idea. He brought Cisco with him when he picked Samantha up from school the next afternoon. Yvonne was driving to Whitebrook in her own car.

"How's your arm?" Samantha asked Tor, looking at the plaster cast that went from the knuckles to the elbow of his left arm.

"It still hurts," Tor said, "but it's better than yesterday. It's annoying to have it in a cast—it gets in the way. So you took Sierra out yesterday after I talked to you?"

"Yeah. I took him around once."

"And you did fine, I'll bet."

"We did okay," Samantha admitted, "though I was pretty nervous. Len said Sierra looked great."

"What we should concentrate on this next week is strategy," Tor said, "especially since Yvonne offered to ride Cisco."

"I've been thinking about that," Samantha agreed.

"We don't know whether Sierra will run better on or off the pace, though. I wish I could just get him in the lead and stay there!"

Tor laughed. "That would be perfect—but the other riders and horses may not cooperate."

"Yeah, I know."

"And riding through a pack of jumpers is a lot more dangerous than squeezing through in a flat race. You'll have to be able to move him in and out of horses, and move him fast in case a horse goes down in front of you—but don't worry," Tor added quickly. "I don't think there will be many falls. The course isn't that difficult."

Samantha was worried enough about getting herself and Sierra cleanly through two and a half miles and sixteen fences. The thought of having to avoid fallen horses and riders at the same time overwhelmed her. "Tor, I don't know if I can do this!"

"Forget I said any of that. I'm jumping ahead too fast. Since we're all so inexperienced, the safest thing to do will be to stay as clear of the rest of the field as you can. That'll probably mean running wide. I'd guess that the other riders will be trying to save ground along the inside rail. Anyway, all you have to think about today is riding clean. Okay?"

Samantha sighed. "I'll try. I haven't said anything to my father yet. Of course, he knows I've been jumping in my lessons with you and riding Sierra here, but I don't know what he's going to say to my riding in an actual steeplechase."

"I think he'll give his okay, Sammy. Explain that

the course won't be any more difficult than what you've been jumping here. He must know what a good horsewoman you are."

"But that's on the flat—and he gave me a hard time when I first wanted to exercise ride for Ashleigh."

"I know he still thinks of your mother's accident," Tor said. "I don't blame him. But that *was* an accident. You've got the skill to ride in the race."

Samantha still felt terribly uncertain about her ability. It was going to take a lot to build up her confidence.

But for all Samantha's worries, the training session went fairly well. With Cisco running next to him, Sierra was showing a preference for wanting to run in the lead. As soon as the other horse started inching up on him, he increased his speed without any urging from Samantha. Samantha was so nervous that she wobbled going over a couple of fences, but in the end, they jumped two full circuits cleanly and in decent time.

Samantha rode off the turf course with Yvonne to see that they had a small audience. Len, Charlie, and Mike were standing with Tor.

"Looking good!" Len called.

"So you're going to have to ride in the race," Mike said. "Tor thinks you'll be able to handle it." Mike didn't sound so sure, and Samantha noticed Charlie shaking his head. He hadn't changed his mind about the foolhardiness of their turning Sierra into a steeplechaser—even after witnessing Sierra's improvement.

"Well—" Samantha began, then seeing Mike's uncertainty, she suddenly felt a new surge of determination. She realized she *wanted* to ride. She wanted to prove that she could do it. "We've got almost two weeks for me to practice," she said. "I'll be ready."

"I just don't want to think of you taking unnecessary risks so Sierra can be in the race."

"She won't be," Tor said quickly. "The course won't be that difficult—no worse than the one she just jumped."

"But there will be other horses to deal with," Mike said.

"I'm used to galloping horses in a small pack," Samantha told him.

"This will be more than a small pack," Mike reminded her, "and a lot more difficult than galloping on the flat. Not that I don't have faith in your riding abilities, but I want you to understand what you're getting into."

"I do," Samantha said firmly.

"Well, you sound pretty determined. Let's hope Sierra stays up to the task. You'll need some silks, Sammy. I'll take care of that. It'll be kind of nice to see Whitebrook's blue and white on a steeplechase course," Mike added.

"If the colt doesn't make fools of you all," Charlie put in brusquely.

Samantha still hadn't said anything to her father about riding, but he found her later in the barn as she was settling Sierra in his stall.

"What's this about your riding in a steeplechase?" he said angrily. "Len just told me. You haven't said anything to me."

Samantha swallowed. "I was going to, Dad, tonight."

"I won't allow it. I know you've been taking jumping lessons, but you don't have enough experience. I don't want you out there breaking your neck."

"I'll be all right, Dad. Tor's the best possible teacher. If we miss this race, we'd have to find another novice steeplechase out of state, and there aren't that many for young horses."

"I know how much you and Tor are counting on this, but I'm not giving my permission. It was one thing when Tor was riding—"

"Dad, I'll be okay!" Samantha said desperately. "Maybe I don't have a lot of experience jumping, but I have tons of experience otherwise. Please don't say I can't! Come out and watch Sierra and me when we practice. You'll see."

"No, Sammy. I can't let you do it. My heart would be in my throat. I'll talk to Mike. There's no reason why he can't wait to race Sierra until Tor can ride again."

"But Mike's thinking of selling Sierra. He said this is Sierra's last chance!"

Her father shook his head. "I'm sorry, but your well-being is more important to me than Sierra's."

"But Dad, it's so important to me. We've worked so hard!"

Her father only shook his head more firmly. "No. I don't want anything to happen to you."

"Nothing *will* happen!" But Samantha knew when her father had made up his mind—and he definitely had. Angry tears welled up in her eyes as her father gave her a stubborn look.

"I'm not doing this to hurt you, Sammy. I'm doing this to protect you. I'll go tell Mike you can't ride. I'll see you in the house for dinner." He turned and walked down the barn aisle.

No! Samantha thought, pressing her head against the stall partition. Just when she had started feeling better about riding, something else had to go wrong. "How can he do this to me, Sierra?" she cried. "He's ruining everything! I'm sixteen years old, and he's still treating me like a baby. It's just not fair!"

Sierra put his head over the stall door and eyed her.

"Oh, I know you don't understand what's going on," she told the colt, "but believe me, it's not good!" She reached out and cautiously patted the colt's nose, then straightened and hurried out of the barn to the cottage.

Tor and Yvonne had already gone home. Samantha rushed upstairs to her bedroom and called Tor.

"Sammy," he said in surprise when he answered. "What's up?"

"My father won't let me ride."

Tor's voice fell. "No—you're kidding."

"He absolutely refused. He said it was too dangerous."

Tor groaned. "You can't get him to change his mind?"

"He's already gone to tell Mike. I just can't believe he'd ruin everything for us."

"Well, you have to think of where he's coming

164

from," Tor said. "I mean, I can understand his being worried. Look, let me talk to him. If we could get him to come watch you take Sierra over the fences, maybe he'd change his mind."

"I doubt it." Samantha plopped down on her bed. "We were supposed to officially enter Sierra in the 'chase this week. Now I'm afraid Mike will just give up without waiting for another steeplechase. How long before you can ride again?"

"Not for weeks, Sammy, maybe longer. I'm sorry."

"There won't be any local 'chases then."

"We'll think of something," Tor said. "Let me talk to your father tomorrow. Don't give up yet."

But Samantha found it pretty hard not to feel desperate. Her father hadn't relented by dinnertime. He tried to make conversation, but Samantha was too angry to talk. She knew she was acting childish, but she couldn't help it.

"Sammy," her father finally said, "it'll work out all right. Mike said he might consider entering Sierra in a later 'chase."

"He *might* consider?" Samantha cried, pushing away from the table. She grabbed her dirty dishes and took them to the sink. When she turned back, her father was gone. She knew her attitude had hurt him, but she was still too angry to care. She went up to her room to call Yvonne.

"I don't believe it," Yvonne said. "After all you and Tor have done with Sierra, how can your father say no now? The race is less than two weeks away."

"Don't remind me. Even if I get him to change his

165

mind—and I doubt I can—it may be too late to enter Sierra anyway."

"Oh, Sammy, I'm sorry."

"So am I."

For two days Samantha was in a miserable mood. Her father didn't show any signs of relenting. Then she overheard Charlie and Len talking in the barn before morning workouts.

"Mike tells me that breeder he met in Florida called him again about Sierra," Charlie said. "He's going to be in Kentucky in a couple of weeks and wants to look at the colt. Guess he's pretty interested in buying him."

"I thought Mike was going to wait and give him a chance in another 'chase when Tor could ride!" Len exclaimed.

"The breeder doesn't want to wait," Charlie answered. "He wants to ship Sierra right to Florida if he likes the look of him. Besides, I still say this steeple-chasing idea is nonsense. That colt's not going to do any better there than he did on the flat. Mike would be foolish not to sell if he got a good offer."

"Sammy's not going to like hearing this, and neither do I," Len said somberly. "Selling him so soon would be a darned shame after all the work she's put in."

Charlie grunted. "Mike's running a business here, remember."

Samantha had instinctively frozen as she listened. Now she felt hot color rush into her cheeks. Mike couldn't sell Sierra without giving him a chance! She spun on her heel and rushed off to Mike's office in the stable. Mike looked up as she stepped into the small room.

"I heard Charlie say a buyer's coming to look at Sierra," Samantha cried. "Please don't sell him yet! I know he can make it as a steeplechaser!"

"Sammy, I'm willing to give him a try," Mike said, "but if this buyer turns out to be interested, he doesn't want to wait."

"But what if I could ride him in the Lexington 'chase?" Samantha asked breathlessly. "Would you still enter him?"

"If you can convince your father to let you ride, sure."

Samantha didn't wait a second longer. She knew her father would be tacking up the horses he would be working that morning. She found him in one of the stalls in the training barn.

The words tumbled out of her mouth as her father turned toward her. "Dad, I just found out Mike might sell Sierra without giving him another chance at steeplechasing!"

"Mike told me," her father said.

"And you don't care?" Samantha cried.

"Of course I care. But I care more about your safety."

Samantha clenched her fists at her sides. "I'll be safe. I can do it. You know I can!"

Her father looked as miserable as she felt. He sighed heavily and ran his hand through his hair. "I've been thinking about this a lot. Tor's talked to me, too. Maybe I'm being too protective a parent again, but you're all I've got—"

"Dad, please! We've worked so hard! Mike said he'd still run Sierra in the Lexington 'chase if I could ride."

"I know you've worked hard, Sammy, and I'm proud of you."

"But it won't be worth anything if Sierra's sold before he can prove himself!" Samantha cried.

Her father was silent for a long moment, staring into the distance. Samantha held her breath.

Finally her father looked back at her. "All right. I'll be an absolute wreck, but I know what a good rider you are. You can ride—I don't want to be responsible for Sierra missing his chance."

Samantha rushed across the stall and gave her father a fierce hug. "Oh, thanks, Dad! Thank you! I know I've been a brat the last couple of days, but it was so important to me."

"You do have a temper, Sammy." Her father smiled wryly. "But that isn't why I changed my mind. I decided you deserve the chance after all your work. Well, what are you waiting for—go call Tor. You've got three days of lost training to make up."

Samantha hugged him again. "I love you, Dad, even when I'm mad at you."

Mr. McLean laughed. "I love you, too."

Samantha hurried to the cottage to call Tor. "All right!" he said ecstatically when she told him the news. "I'll be over this afternoon when you get home from school. We've got work to do! After all we've been through, we can't blow it now!"

15

YVONNE WATCHED AS SAMANTHA PACKED THE BAG SHE would take to the steeplechase course. "I'm so nervous I can hardly think!" Samantha said as she carefully folded the blue-and-white silks Mike had given her. She put them in her canvas carryall with her hard hat and freshly polished boots. Then she looked around distractedly. "What else do I need?"

"Relax!" Yvonne told her. "Look how well you and Sierra have done in the past two weeks. You're both jumping great, and you said Tor timed you at a little over four minutes for two miles. That sounds pretty good to me. He's set, and so are you."

"I'm worried about the crowds. Who knows how Sierra will react? And what if I fall and make a fool out of myself? What if I ruin everything for Sierra?"

"You're not going to fall. You haven't fallen yet over the fences here."

That was true, although Samantha knew she'd

come close a couple of times—but not in the last week. "I guess I'm set," she said, zipping her bag and heaving a sigh. "Len and Tor should have Sierra ready to go."

The girls headed out of the McLeans' cottage and across the yard. The weather at least was cooperating. The late April sky was nearly cloudless, and the temperature was a comfortable seventy degrees. Everyone was gathered around Mike's two-horse van as Len led Sierra out of the stable. The colt looked good. His liver chestnut coat was gleaming, and there was a spring in his step. "I just hope Sierra behaves himself today," Samantha said, chewing her lip.

"He's been pretty good for a while," Yvonne reminded her.

"That doesn't necessarily mean anything with him."

When they reached the others, Tor immediately came to Samantha's side and slung his arm around her shoulders. "How're you doing?" he asked. His other arm was healing, but it was still encased in plaster and bothered him if he put any stress on it.

"I could be better," Samantha answered.

"At least Sierra's race goes off first," Yvonne said. "So you won't have all afternoon to wait and get more nervous."

Samantha noticed that her father looked as nervous as she felt, even though he'd been somewhat reassured after watching her work with Sierra in the last week. "You're sure you're all set, Sammy?" he asked worriedly.

"As set as I can be, Dad."

"I remember how I felt before I rode in my first race," Ashleigh said. "I was a real basket case, but once I was out on the track, I was able to concentrate and forget about everything else. It'll be the same for you, Sammy."

Samantha gave Ashleigh a weak smile and nodded.

"I just hope that colt holds together," Charlie said brusquely. "The crowds and the noise aren't going to help."

That wasn't the kind of comment Samantha wanted her father to hear—she didn't particularly want to hear it herself. She scowled at Charlie in warning. Mike and Len had finished loading Sierra in the van, and Mike called over, "Ready to go, guys?"

Mr. McLean gave Samantha a parting hug. He'd volunteered to stay at Whitebrook to keep an eye on things, since he didn't think he could stand the tension of watching the race. "Good luck," he said to Samantha.

"Thanks, Dad, and don't worry. We'll be all right."

"I hope so. Just don't take any unnecessary risks, Sammy."

"I won't. I promise."

Samantha went to the van and climbed in the front seat between Mike and Tor. Ashleigh had offered to drive the others over in her car. Samantha heard Sierra snort from his stall in the rear of the van, but he was used to van rides, and Samantha knew the trip wouldn't upset him. Mike started the engine, and they were rolling out the drive of

171

Whitebrook, with Ashleigh following in her car.

Tor and Samantha had driven over to have a look at the steeplechase course during the week. The hedged, mile-long, turf-covered oval, and the acres of lawns and trees surrounding it, had been quiet then. Samantha knew that wouldn't be the case today. The six-race steeplechase meet would draw a huge crowd, especially since the weather was perfect.

They weren't the first competitors to arrive. Horse vans covered one large field. Mike followed the attendant's directions and parked at the end of a row. As they got out of the van, Samantha looked across toward the course itself. Already the crowd was thick on the lawns, and the first chase wouldn't start for several hours.

"We'd better check in with the race officials," Tor said.

"Let me take care of it," Mike offered. "I'll be back in a few minutes."

Samantha decided to take Sierra out of the van and walk him around. It would give him a chance to get used to the crowds—and give her something to take her mind off her nervousness.

The colt's ears pricked and he snorted uncertainly when Samantha had backed him from the van. He turned his head from side to side, eyeing the commotion, then skittered his hindquarters in an arc. Samantha took a firmer hold on the lead shank. "Just take it easy, Sierra," she said softly. "It's okay."

The colt continued to prance excitedly, and Samantha laid a reassuring hand on his sleek shoulder as Len walked over. "He'll settle down in due course," he said. "You might want to walk him."

"Yeah, I was going to. A walk might do me good, too," Samantha said. Her stomach was flip-flopping like crazy.

"I think the rest of us should find a spot to sit while we still can," Ashleigh suggested.

"Sounds like a good idea to me," Charlie said. "From the looks of it, we'll be lucky if we can get a clear view of the track. Sure not like a regular track with grandstand seating," he grumbled.

Ashleigh smiled at the old trainer. "Just enjoy yourself, Charlie. It's a beautiful day. There's plenty of sun, and we've got your deck chair in the trunk."

"Hmph. I can't even see where they start and finish on this course. Don't they use a starting gate?"

"No, they drop a flag at the start," Samantha answered. "The starting line will be somewhere near the officials' stand."

Charlie shook his head. Len and Yvonne had collected several deck chairs and a cooler from the trunk of Ashleigh's car. "I'll come back when I've helped them set up," Yvonne told Samantha.

Samantha nodded.

"And I'll wait here at the van for Mike," Tor said, easing himself down on the tailgate.

"Your arm's bothering you, isn't it?" Samantha asked with concern.

"A little. But don't worry about me. Get Sierra walked."

As the others headed off to find a spot to sit,

173

Samantha led Sierra toward the end of the field where there was the least congestion. The colt was huffing and snorting. He definitely wasn't settling down.

"Please be a good boy today, Sierra," Samantha pleaded. "I'm going to be so nervous, I don't know if I'll be able to handle any craziness from you."

The colt just gave another snort and tossed his head. Samantha studied the other horses that were being walked. She had no idea what horses would be in their race. And there would be five other races run, all for more experienced horses. She saw some beautiful animals. And she noticed that Sierra was getting his own share of admiring glances—or maybe people were noticing him because of his high-strung behavior.

Yvonne was waiting when Samantha led Sierra back to the van, and Mike had returned with the numbered saddlecloth Sierra would wear.

"He's number nine, way on the outside," Tor told Samantha, "which is probably the best place for you to be."

"Doesn't look like he's calmed down much," Mike said with a frown.

"No, I'm afraid he hasn't," Samantha said. "He's not used to all this excitement."

"There's time yet," Tor said. "We don't have to get down to the saddling area until half an hour before the race." Tor handed Samantha a program. "Here's the field for his race. Ten horses."

Samantha looked at the program and the past performance records for each horse in their race.

"Sierra's the only one who hasn't raced before!" she cried. "And the only three-year-old!"

Tor tried to reassure her. "We have to start somewhere, Sammy, and remember, this is a real amateur field. They may be more experienced, but if they'd been performing really well, they probably wouldn't be entered in this race."

"Oh, God, I wish you were riding!"

"Don't get cold feet now," Tor said. "You can do it!"

But Samantha didn't feel any better an hour later. She had changed into her silks in the van, with Yvonne chattering away beside her. Samantha knew her friend was trying to distract her from her worries, but it wasn't working. As they set out to the saddling area, Samantha led Sierra, and Mike carried Sierra's saddle. Weight would be added to the saddle—because Sierra was a three-year-old, he would carry less than the rest of the field.

When they got to the saddling area, several other horses were already there. Most of them didn't look very impressive to Samantha's practiced eye, but she knew looks didn't necessarily mean anything. There were a few horses that looked like fit athletes, and all of them were behaving more calmly than Sierra. Sierra had tried to take a bite out of Tor before they'd led him down, and now he was beginning to break out in a sweat.

Tor and Mike held the colt as Samantha took the saddle and saddlecloth to the officials' stand to be weighed in. She waited while an official inserted extra weight bars in the saddle. Then, with the saddle in her arms, she stepped up on the big scales. The needle stopped at one hundred and thirty-eight pounds.

She saw the other riders in her race looking at her curiously. There was only one other woman. All the other riders were men, and all of them were bigger and stronger than Samantha.

The woman smiled at Samantha. "I haven't seen you at any meets before. I'm Amy."

"Hi. I'm Samantha. This is my first race."

One of the male riders glanced at the number on Samantha's saddlecloth. "Number nine, huh? You're riding that maiden three-year-old."

"Yes."

"They shouldn't allow three-year-olds in these races," someone else muttered. "They're always green as heck. I'll make sure I stay out of their way."

"Two maidens. They'll probably fall at the first fence anyway," another jockey said under his breath, but loud enough for Samantha to hear.

"Don't pay any attention to them," Amy told Samantha. "They're just trying to rattle you."

They had succeeded in doing that! Samantha felt her confidence evaporating totally as she walked back to Tor and Mike. And seeing Sierra prancing and throwing his head up against the lead shank didn't help. She felt close to fainting as she watched Mike saddle Sierra. *Maybe it would be a good thing if I did faint*, she thought. *Then I wouldn't have to ride.*

Tor saw her expression. "Sammy, what is it?" He quickly put his good arm around her shoulders.

Weakly she repeated what the other jockeys had said.

"They don't know what they're talking about. Sierra's never raced, but *you* know he can get over these fences, and you can do it, too. In fact, he'll probably kick dirt in their faces."

Mike was looking at her with concern. "Tor's right. Don't listen to the other jockeys. You know your horse."

Samantha nodded. She hated herself for falling apart like this. They'd worked so hard toward this moment!

"Just stay clear of the traffic," Tor said. "You shouldn't have too much trouble doing that, since you're starting from the nine position. There'll only be one horse outside of you. Take it easy and slow. Think about each fence as it comes, not the whole course."

"Sammy," Mike added, "if you really feel that uncertain, we don't have to race."

"No," Samantha said, drawing a deep breath into her lungs. "I'm going to do it!"

"Okay. Then give it your best shot."

There was no more time for talk. The riders were being given the signal to mount. Tor held Sierra as Mike gave Samantha a leg into the saddle. She settled herself and gathered the reins. Tor reached up and squeezed Samantha's hand. "Good luck. In my mind, I'll be out on that course with you."

Samantha managed a weak smile. She used every ounce of willpower to pull herself together and focus her mind. She and Sierra were going to go out there and jump that course. They probably wouldn't win, but she was going to make sure they finished—and finished well enough for Mike to acknowledge Sierra's ability!

She followed the other riders onto the course and jogged with them as they warmed up the horses. She had all she could do to keep Sierra in hand. He was totally confused by the large field and the noise and commotion of the spectators. "Easy, boy," she said soothingly. "I know it's strange. Just make believe we're back at Whitebrook."

The colt wasn't responding to her words, and when it came time to line up for the start, Samantha couldn't get Sierra to steady. His feet churned beneath him as he tried to plunge forward past the line. He eyed the horse next to him and would have snaked his head out to bite if Samantha had allowed him the extra rein.

Samantha heard the rider next to her snigger. Then suddenly the starting flag was dropped. With all her efforts focused on trying to steady Sierra, Samantha wasn't prepared. The rest of the field jumped out and left them on the line. "Go, Sierra!" Samantha shouted urgently, kneading her hands along his neck. Only then did he wake up and lunge out after the field.

"What an awful start!" Samantha moaned, feeling close to tears. But Sierra was galloping strongly now, determined to catch the horses in front of him. Samantha wasn't about to give up either. She put her mind on the task ahead. She focused her eyes on the first fence. The leaders were already clearing it, but Sierra was gaining ground, and as they approached the fence he was up even with the last few horses. Samantha held him outside of the others. He made a powerful leap, gaining another half-stride going over the fence. They landed and galloped off.

Sierra's ears were back, listening to her commands. He was interested, and that might be half the battle won. But they had most of the race still ahead of them, Samantha reminded herself. She and Sierra roared on toward the next fence. They'd already passed three horses in the field and were gaining on a fourth. Samantha had eased Sierra in slightly toward the middle of the course. She saw the leaders clearing the fence ahead in a bunch, but she and Sierra were running clear. There was only one horse inside of them. She prepared Sierra. He thrust with his hindquarters, and they lifted. They were in midair over the fence when the horse inside of them careened over into them, hitting Sierra's shoulder with his own.

The bump jarred Samantha and Sierra badly. She felt Sierra twisting away from the impact, gamely trying to collect himself and bring them down safely on the other side of the fence. But, short of a miracle, Samantha knew there was no way Sierra could land evenly after such a bad bump.

Sierra's front feet hit the ground. Samantha was flung up on his neck as he went down to his knees. *Oh, no!* Samantha thought. *We're finished—after only two fences!* She envisioned the colt going head over heels. From the corner of her eye, she saw that the horse inside of them, who had caused the collision, was down.

But somehow, Sierra had gotten his hindquarters under him and was gallantly straightening his forelegs. In the next instant he was up, and they were galloping away from the fence. Samantha couldn't believe it, but all her energy was directed to steadying herself and Sierra. She shoved her heels down in her stirrups and rebalanced herself in the saddle. It took several strides before she was in control again and Sierra regained his momentum. They had lost a lot of ground, and a horse passed them on the inside. But Sierra was not about to give up.

"You're something, boy!" Samantha breathlessly cried. "That's the way! We'll show Mike!"

As they approached the next fence, Samantha held Sierra well to the outside. Then they were over, passing the horse that had just passed them. Sierra's hooves dug into the turf. He and Samantha were working like a team, and Samantha no longer had room in her mind for fear.

They continued gaining ground as they came down the backstretch. They'd passed half the field, but the lead horses were still many lengths in front. Sierra strove to increase his speed between the fences, but Samantha didn't want him to use up too much when they still had another circuit to go. Another horse went down at the eighth fence, but because Samantha had kept Sierra well to the outside, they had no problems avoiding the fallen horse and rider.

They swept past the finish for the first time. Samantha heard the faint roar of the crowd. The best she could judge was that they were in fifth, but she only had a clear view of the field ahead when they were in the air over a fence. The leaders still looked like they were bunched, and she and Sierra had a good ten lengths to make up to catch them.

Sierra was still fighting for rein, and as they landed off the next jump Samantha let him have it. He powered them forward between the fences. His leaps over the fences were long and powerful. With four fences still to go, they surged past another rider.

"You're doing good, boy! Wonderful!" Samantha cried, though she doubted Sierra could hear her over the pounding of his hooves and the even snort of his breaths. He knew there were horses in front of him, though, and he was determined to catch them. When they landed off the next fence, Samantha saw the leaders were only about six lengths ahead now. One of the horses was tiring and starting to drift wide, right in Sierra's path. Samantha had no choice but to move Sierra in closer to the middle of the track, even if it meant they would have horses to either side of them. Sierra gained another length on the two leaders over the next fence, and with powerful strides, moved up on them even more between fences.

Two more fences to go, Samantha thought. *We can do it. We can prove to Mike you've got what it takes.* With Sierra continually pulling them forward, they were on the heels of the leaders approaching the last fence. Sierra was showing his class. Even if their chances of

181

winning were slim, Samantha was amazed that the colt had been able to make up so much ground. And he was doing it on his own!

Sierra was forging through the gap between the two leaders, still a half-length behind, but rapidly closing on them. They were two strides from the fence when one of the leaders swerved in, narrowing the gap. Samantha nearly panicked. She'd be elbow to elbow with the two other jockeys going over the fence, but it was too late to change Sierra's course. And he had no intention of changing course anyway. Without hesitation, he surged into the narrow opening, thrust with his hindquarters, lifted, and soared. Samantha could have reached out and touched the horses and jockeys on either side of them. But when they landed, they were a half-length in the lead!

Samantha gasped. "My gosh! We're going to win it!" She couldn't believe it. Then she saw there was yet another horse and rider ahead. Her view of them had been blocked by the horses Sierra had just passed. And Samantha didn't think there was any way she and Sierra could catch the leader now, with only one fence to go.

"Let's *try* to get them, anyway!" she called to Sierra. She gave him the rein he wanted, and they roared over the grass out of the turn toward the last fence. The horse in the lead was going over it, but they still had the stretch drive toward the finish. Sierra gathered, leaped, and cleared the last fence. Samantha set him down for the drive home. Now she had every confidence in what she was doing. This was no different than a stretch drive on the flat. She crouched low over Sierra's neck and kneaded her hands along his neck. "Let's get 'em, big guy!"

Sierra responded. Even after the two miles of jumps, he still had something left. With each stride he was gaining on the leader, but Samantha could see they would run out of ground by the wire. There was just too much distance for Sierra to make up. Still, Sierra had his head level with the other horse's flank as they swept past the finish. They'd come in second. After all the problems they'd had, Sierra had still managed to get up for a close second. It was unbelievable. What an incredible performance Sierra had put in—making up so much ground after a bad start and a near fall!

Samantha stood in her stirrups and began pulling Sierra up. She felt heady and as elated as if they'd won. Mike couldn't have any doubts now that he had a steeplechaser in his stable! She excitedly patted Sierra's neck. "Good boy!" she crooned. "You were wonderful—absolutely terrific. I couldn't ask for more!"

The colt responded by arching his neck and giving his head a little toss.

Samantha started circling Sierra back. By now the rest of the field were finishing and cantering up the track. Several of the other jockeys cast amazed and mystified looks in Samantha and Sierra's direction. A moment later, the winning jockey rode up beside Samantha. It was the same man who'd made the most stinging comments about their chances and had sniggered at them on the starting line.

"Guess I have to eat my words," he said tersely. "I don't know how you did it. This must have been your lucky day."

"Sierra did it with heart and courage," Samantha said, getting a little revenge for what his earlier words had done to her.

The winning jockey frowned and rode off to collect his honors. As Samantha trotted Sierra off the track Tor, Yvonne, Mike, Ashleigh, and Len eagerly rushed up. Charlie shuffled along a few paces behind. Samantha saw the brilliant sparkle of happiness in Tor's blue eyes, and she smiled back at him.

"What a race!" Mike cried. "Unbelievable the ground he made up. I thought you were goners when you got bumped on that second fence."

"The colt showed courage, all right," Charlie muttered reluctantly. "Guess I was wrong about this steeplechasing idea."

"Sammy," Mike added sincerely, "you did an incredible job out there. All I can say is that you and Tor have given me hopes for Sierra I never would have had otherwise."

"Does that mean you want to keep steeplechasing him? You won't sell him?" Samantha asked breathlessly.

Mike laughed. "Are you kidding? After what he did today, I'd be out of my mind not to keep running him!"

"All right!" Yvonne cried.

Tor held Sierra as Samantha dismounted. She stepped over to join him at Sierra's head. She took

Sierra's muzzle and kissed his velvet nose. "You did it, boy. Finally, you've shown your stuff." Then Samantha looked up at Tor. His smile totally melted her already wobbly knees.

"See what you can do when you put your mind to it?" he said. "You always believed in Sierra."

Samantha sighed happily. "Yes—at least most of the time."

"And it only gets better from here," Tor said. He took her hand and squeezed it. Sierra gave a breathy snort of approval.

Joanna Campbell was born and raised in Norwalk, Connecticut, with her three younger brothers. When she was a child, she owned her own horse, Moe, a chestnut part Quarter Horse. In her early twenties, she took open jumping lessons and competed in cross-country point-to-points. Still an avid horse fan, she recently saw the Breeders' Cup races in Belmont Park, New York. She is the author of twenty-six young adult novels, and four adult novels. She now lives in Camden, Maine, with her husband, Ian Bruce, their dog, Preppie, and their cat, Kiki. She has two children, Kimberly and Kenneth, and three grandchildren, Taylor, Kyle, and Becca.